j   39583

Clark
       Magic money.

Magic Money

Also by Ann Nolan Clark

A story of a country boy
who lives in Costa Rica
in Central America

MAGIC MONEY

by Ann Nolan Clark

Illustrated by Leo Politi

New York · THE VIKING PRESS · 1950

Set in Caledonia and Bernhard Modern Bold types
and lithographed in the United States of America
by Affiliated Lithographers, Inc.

Contents

1. Tony's Secret

TONY had a secret. It was not a secret not-to-tell. It was a secret wanting. It was something Tony wanted. He wanted something very much. From the first day that he had wanted this something, it had been big. It lived with Tony every day because he kept thinking about it. At night he dreamed about it.

Last night he dreamed it came true. In his dream he walked down the road to tell Grandpapa.

But that was last night and that was a dream. This morning Tony sat on the doorstep of his house. He thought about last night's dream. All around him was the wide porch of his house. Tony did not call it a porch. Tony called it *corredor*. That is the Costa Rican Spanish word and all the words that Tony uses are Costa Rican Spanish. On one side of the corredor the wood was piled high. On the other side was his Papa's painted ox-cart. From the corredor roof bright flower plants in hanging tin baskets made a curtain above him.

Outside the trees came close to the house. They came close, close, close, as if they were pushing nearer and nearer to look through the windows of Tony's house.

It was a beautiful world where Tony lived. There were trees and flowers and vines and ferns all tangled up together around the little house. The road was a narrow red-brown ribbon with bright green edges, winding through the tall grass among the trees.

Tony did not see these things. Tony was thinking. Big rain drops splashed on the leaves of the coffee tree, slipping tiny fingers down to the grasses that were stretching up to touch them. Soon the raindrops would come thicker and faster, for now was the rainy time of year. Every day it rained.

Mama called to the little boy sitting on the doorstep thinking of his dream. Mama called, "Manuel Antonio, come in. We are eating breakfast."

Tony went into the house. He sat at the table with his Mama and his Papa, his brother Roberto, and his sister Maria Rosita. They all were much bigger than Tony. Tony was the youngest in his family. Today he did not feel like the youngest. Today he felt grown-up. He felt important. He had a secret. He wanted to talk about his secret. He did not want to tell what it was. He wanted to find out how to get it.

Mama poured coffee in Tony's cup. She poured hot milk into

the coffee and sweetened it with broken bits of brown sugar. Tony liked brown sugar very much. He called it *dulce*. He said, "Please, Mama, put more *dulce* in my coffee." Mama put a tortilla on Tony's plate. Tony liked tortillas too. They were such good, big, round, flat corncakes, Tony could not help but like them. He said, "Please, Mama, put more tortillas on my plate." Mama also put little hills of black beans and of white rice on Tony's plate. It was a good breakfast. Tony was hungry.

Papa was talking. He said, "Yes, if our Rosita wants to go to San José to work in the house of the rich Niña Lygia, I can see no harm in it. Remember, Mama, our daughter is as good as she is beautiful."

Tony looked at his sister Maria Rosita. Yes. She was beautiful. He could see it. Her face was lovely and so creamy white. Her cheeks were so red and her hair and her eyes were so black and so shining.

Mama pushed her breakfast plate away. Her words came fast and close together. Tony looked at her. She was excited. She was not pleased about something. She told Papa, "Yes, yes, she is good. I know that. It is also time that our beautiful Maria Rosita should work in the city that she may know its ways. But there is something else, Papa. Surely you must know that she cannot just go to San José. There is something else."

Mama went to her little clay stove. She pushed a stick of wood under the coffee pot. Smoke curled up along the white walls. To Tony it smelled like rice and beans and coffee. It smelled good.

Roberto, the big brother, laughed. "She is trying to tell you something, Papa. Our little Mama is trying to tell you that the charming one needs something that you must buy before she can go to San José."

Mama came back to the table. She stood beside Maria Rosita. She smiled at Roberto. She smiled at Papa. She waited.

"Oh, oh," said Papa, "I should have known that. It is a ribbon, perhaps? A ribbon for her hair? Does she need a little ribbon?"

"No, no," Roberto told him. "She has a ribbon. I myself gave her one for her Name-Day Feast."

Papa said, "Well, maybe an apron then?"

Mama said, "No. Maria Rosita has an apron."

Papa pushed his plate away. He began to talk fast, very fast. "You have a ribbon. You have an apron. You have a dress. What more can you want to go to San José?"

Maria Rosita answered him. She spoke softly. She smiled shyly at him. "Shoes," she told him. "I want shoes to wear."

Papa was surprised. Roberto was surprised. Even Tony was surprised. He almost forgot to keep on taking bites of rice and beans.

Papa said, "Shoes! It is shoes you want! Times have changed since I was young."

Rosita said, "Yes, Papa."

Roberto said, "They will hurt your feet. I have heard it said. Shoes hurt the feet."

Papa said, "I think you won't like them."

Rosita said, "I want them."

"Well," Roberto told her, "I think they won't want you."

But Maria Rosita only laughed. "I want shoes to wear to San José."

After more talking, Papa said, "All right. If you want shoes you may have shoes. Today I will take our pig to market. I will sell him there. When I come back I will bring money for your Mama to buy you shoes."

Mama and Maria Rosita were happy. They began to laugh and

sing and to dance around the room. Roberto and Papa laughed at them. "That is what happens to beautiful women," Papa told Roberto. "They want shoes."

Papa got up from the breakfast table. "Roberto, please, before you go to the Patron's house to work for him, get the oxen in from the field. I will need them and my ox-cart to take the pig to market and to bring home the money for shoes for our beautiful Rosita."

Papa went out of the door. He went to get the pig. He was still laughing. Mama laughed too. "Your Papa is a good man," she told her children. Then she said to Maria Rosita, "Run, my charming one, and put some bananas in the ox-cart for Papa to sell at market."

She told Tony, "Tonito, run quickly with this little tin bucket to find eggs that are in the nests in the long grass. Papa can take them to sell at market."

Mama thought for a minute. "Can I spare a hen to sell? Yes. Perhaps a very thin one. Papa can sell it at market, too."

Roberto put a big banana leaf over his shoulders for a raincoat. He rolled up the legs of his trousers. He got ready for work.

Roberto was important. He worked for the Patron. Every morning he milked all of the Patron's cows. He put the milk in two large cans tied to the saddle of the horse he rode. Then he would ride off on the horse with his two large cans of milk. He rode horseback to San José. Roberto was a milkman. Milkmen have important work to do. If it were not for them, the rich people of the city would not have milk to drink. Being a milkman was Roberto's job. He worked for money.

Tony went to stand beside his brother before he went outside to hunt for eggs. "How tall am I now, Roberto? Am I as tall as you are—almost?"

"You are about as tall as my milk can, Little One. A little taller, maybe."

Tony sighed. He was still little. He was not big enough to work in San José.

"What is the matter?" Roberto wanted to know. Roberto was a good brother.

"I have a secret," Tony answered.

"Aha! A secret! Can you tell me?"

"It is not a telling secret. It is a wanting secret. It is something that I want. It is something that I want for someone."

"Can you find it?"

"No. It is not a thing that can be found."

"Can you make it?"

"No. It is not a thing that can be made."

"Is it something that must be bought?"

"Yes."

"That makes it difficult. To buy things takes money. Did you know that?"

"Yes."

"Money is hard to get, but when you get it—pooff—" Roberto snapped his fingers. "It is magic!" Roberto laughed. "Someday, some way, maybe you will get that something that you want." Roberto laughed again. He went out the door to get the oxen. Then he would go to the house of the Patron. Roberto had work to do.

Tony stopped at the table to eat the last bite of what was left of the little hills of beans and rice on his breakfast plate. He drank the last drop of coffee and milk and *dulce* in his coffee cup. This done, breakfast was finished. Now he could go to hunt the eggs.

When he came back, the ox-cart and the oxen were standing

before the house door. The ox-cart was almost full. Papa had tied the fat, squealing pig in one corner. Mama had tied two hens, both thin, to the end board. Maria Rosita had put in a bunch of big green bananas and a few pineapples and a can of shelled peas picked fresh from the little garden behind the house.

Mama said, "All this to sell at market!"

"But remember," Papa told her, "only the pig money is for the shoes."

Now Papa was ready. Everything was in the ox-cart. Papa said good-by. He walked in front of his oxen down the little narrow road to far-off San José.

Mama and her daughter and her son went into the house.

Mama and Rosita began to wash the clothes in the cement tub.

They filled the tub with water. They rubbed the soaped clothes against the rough stone bottom of the tub. They talked as they worked. They talked about San José and about working there. They talked about wearing shoes.

Outside the morning rain came down like water pouring from a pitcher. The ground and the grass were wet. The flowers and the trees were wet. The air was heavy and filled with silver rain.

Tony stood at the door and looked out at the raining world. He thought about his secret. It made him feel strange to have such a big secret inside him.

Mama stopped washing the clothes. She stopped talking to Maria Rosita. She came to stand beside her little boy. She put her wet hand on his shoulder. "Go to see Grandpapa. Your poor Grandpapa! Now that his old ox is dead, he is very lonely."

"I know," Tony answered. "I am thinking of Grandpapa. Now he has no oxen to pull his beautiful painted ox-cart. I will go to visit him. Maybe he can tell me how to get the secret."

"You have a secret, my Tony?"

"Yes, Mama, a secret."

"Can you tell me?"

"No, Mama, not until I am ready to get it."

"You will get it, Tonito. I feel it in my heart. You will get your secret someday."

Tony went down the red-brown ribbon of road under the tall trees. The rain spattered him, but gently now. It was not heavy, now. It was not cold. It was only wet.

Tony's bare feet went slushing in the mud of the road. He and his secret were going to his grandfather's house. "I will tell Grandpapa a little about my secret," he thought as he walked along. "This Grandpapa of mine can help me. I know it."

2. Money Is Important

RANDPAPA's house was like Tony's house. All the workers' houses on the coffee plantation were alike. They were painted pink, with blue doors and blue windows and sloping red tile roofs. The Patron who owned the plantation and the houses on it liked the color pink. He liked pink houses. He liked his workmen to have pretty, neat, clean houses to live in.

Grandpapa's house was very clean. Even though he was old and lived alone and had to do his own housework, everything was always clean. When Mama and Maria Rosita came to help him they said, "Ay! Ay! There is nothing to do here. The old one cleans it as well as we can do it."

Now Tony came up on the wide corredor. He saw Grandpapa's high woodpile on one side. He saw Grandpapa's beautiful painted ox-cart on the other side. Now that his last old ox was dead, Grandpapa would not be taking his beautiful ox-cart to the mill where the brown sugar was made.

Tony quietly opened the blue door and went inside the house. Grandpapa was sitting in a chair by the window. He had eaten his breakfast and washed his breakfast cup and plate. He had swept the floor and spread his straw mat and his blanket neatly across his wide plank bed. He heard Tony and turned his great white head to see him.

"Good morning, Little One. It is good to see you. Now that I go no more to work at the brown sugar mill the day becomes as long as it is quiet."

He patted Tony's small black head. "You are welcome, Grandson. Come in. Come in. My house is yours."

Tony came into the room. He sat politely on the little box near the clay stove. "I see you have beans cooking, Grandpapa, and the coffee is still dripping from the coffee bag."

"Yes," the old man answered. "It is not so long since the breakfast hour."

"About that ox of yours, Grandpapa. I want to tell you. Perhaps someday another one will be given to you."

"Perhaps, Tonito, but I am old and money to buy oxen is hard to come by. But we are wasting time. Let us wash my ox-cart as I have always done each day."

The young boy and the old man went to the washing place on the corredor. They got water there to fill their buckets. They began to scrub the big two-wheeled, brightly painted cart. It did not need to be washed. It was clean. There was no mud on its wheels. To Tony its cleanliness said, "I am of no use now to this old man who loves me. There are no oxen to pull me. I do not work for this old one any more." Tony's tears splashed into his water bucket as he worked. He kept his face turned away. Grandpapa must not know that his grandson was crying.

The old man talked as he scrubbed the cart sides and the great wooden wheels. If he too saw that they were clean because they were not used, he did not say it. He did not cry. He scrubbed the cart wheels. He talked of other things.

"This cart is very beautiful even though I myself say it. Twice, Manuel Antonio, twice, mind you, I have won the grand prize at the cart parade in San José."

"The design is very beautiful, Grandpapa."

"Yes. It is my design. Even for my home village of San Ramón, where ox-carts were among the first to be painted, it is a beautiful design. All ox-carts are beautiful, Little One. Every province has its special kind of painted decorations. I am old, but still I can tell in what province an ox-cart has been painted just by the kind of design it has."

Grandpapa stopped to rest. So much scrubbing and so much talking had made him tired. He looked quickly at Tony to see if the boy could tell that he was a little tired. No. It was all right. Tony's face was turned away. He was not looking at his Grandpapa.

Grandpapa was rested now. He began to scrub the cart again. He began to talk again.

"I myself like the flower design to be painted on the carts. I like very much my own, this beautiful purple orchid, the flower of our lovely country, Manuel Antonio."

Tony's tears had stopped. He smiled at Grandpapa. He felt like talking now that he did not need to turn his face away. "Tell me about the cart parade in San José, Grandpapa. Always I have wanted to see it. Sometimes being little is too hard for a young boy. Roberto who is big has been to see the ox-cart parade."

"Your day will come, Tonito. If I had my two white oxen, we would go this year. It is a very gay fiesta. All the country people from all the provinces of the highlands of Costa Rica bring their beautiful ox-carts and their beautiful oxen and make a parade in the city streets. San José is a lovely city and more so at fiesta time. The streets are decorated with crepe-paper flowers and crepe-paper chains and crepe-paper ropes and silken banners. The ladies are very gay in the old time dresses of our country. Even the rich are so dressed."

Grandpapa stopped. He was thinking back to that happy time

when he had walked before his oxen through the streets of San José in the fiesta parade.

"Your Mama would ride in the ox-cart and her sister with her. Do not forget, my Tonito, that the ladies of Costa Rica are the most beautiful in the world, and your Mama was more beautiful than any other."

"Was she as beautiful as Maria Rosita, Grandpapa?"

"Ay! Ay! More beautiful, although the charming Rosita fills my heart with pride."

This made Tony remember the news about Rosita. His eyes twinkled up at Grandpapa through the thick tangle of his long eyelashes. "Now I remember to tell you. Maria Rosita is going to the city to work for the Patron's sister Niña Lygia. Papa will buy shoes for her to wear."

"Shoes? Rosita will have shoes? Where will your Papa get the money to buy Rosita shoes?"

"He is selling the pig."

"Oh! That pig is a good one. Better than shoes, I would say, but I am old and times change. Is Papa going to pick coffee for the Patron this year?"

"Yes. Tomorrow Mama will take Rosita to the market at San José to buy the shoes. Then Rosita will stay in the city to work. The next day Papa and Mama will pick the coffee berries for the Patron."

"That is good. It is good to work, and to work for money is a thing we must do these days when we must buy so many things."

"Grandpapa," Tony's voice was low. His secret had come back again. Now it felt like a lump in his throat. He must tell some of it. Of course, not all of it. He must have help to learn how to get such a big thing.

"Grandpapa, Grandpapa, I have a secret."

"A secret, Grandson? A secret must not be told."

"No, Grandpapa. But I want something. It is not for me. It is for someone else. I must buy it."

Tony stopped. He looked at his Grandpapa, at the wrinkled face, at the kind black eyes.

"Grandpapa, I must buy it. Where then can I get the money for this thing? How does one get money, my Grandpapa? Tell me."

"Money is difficult to get, Manuel Antonio."

"Yes, but money is important. I have seen it. When my Mama wanted a washtub so she would not need to go to the river to wash our clothes, Papa worked for money. I remember. He worked, and then he had money to buy cement to make the tub."

"Yes. That is true. That is the way I got my washtub."

"And, Grandpapa, when Roberto wanted a guitar, he worked for the Patron, and pooff—just like that he got money, and with his money he got the guitar."

Tony snapped his fingers and raised his eyebrows and his shoulders as he had seen Roberto do. "Pooff—just like that," he said.

"Yes. That is also true. A beautiful guitar if there ever was one."

"And now, Grandpapa, there are these shoes for my sister Rosita. Money today, shoes tomorrow. Do you understand what I mean? Money is important."

"Yes, Tonito. I understand. Money is important when you have it, and yes, perhaps it is even more important when you do not have it. Yes, Little One, I understand you. Money is important."

"But where to get it, Grandpapa? I have seen it, but it has not been mine. I myself have not had money."

"Well, you could work perhaps."

"But I am young to work."

"Yes, you are young, but it could be that you could do a little work. I think, anyway, that you could try."

Grandpapa stopped to think. He sat on a box near his painted cart. His thinking was deep and quiet.

Outside the rain came down slowly. It dropped from the sloping roof—a drop and a drop and a drop. It was as if each drop waited to hear what Grandpapa could think of for work that a young boy could do.

Far away a dog barked faintly, and a bird called to another bird out where the bananas hung heavy from the broad-leaved stalks.

Would Grandpapa think of something? Tony waited. He did not speak. He could not have spoken if he had wanted to. The secret wanting inside his heart was so big, so very big. He had to make it come true. Somewhere, some way, someday, he had to get some money magic to make his dream come true.

Then Grandpapa spoke. He spoke slowly, doubtfully. "Well, perhaps, it just might be possible that the Patron would give you money if you helped your Mama and your Papa pick coffee berries. Perhaps."

"Oh! Oh! Grandpapa, what a wonderful idea. Will my Papa let me, do you think?"

"He may. Come. I will go with you to see your Mama. If your Mama says yes, your Papa will say yes. I know how it is."

"Will our Patron let me, do you think?"

"The Patron will not care. He pays for coffee berries picked. It does not matter who picks them. Then, too, he is a good man. Our Patron is of the best. Come. We will go."

The old man and the young boy went down the narrow ribbon of road that wound among the tall trees. They went back to Tony's house.

Now the rain had stopped. The sun shone and even the clouds pushed away and piled up at one end of the sky. They were hiding the face of the old volcano. Birds sang softly. Flowers nodded brightly at Grandpapa and Tonito as they passed by.

"I will work. I will make money. I will buy something for somebody that you and I know. That is my secret. That is my secret."

Tony put his hand into his Grandpapa's big one. "My secret and I will come walking down the road to you, my Grandpapa," Tony chatted as he tried to stretch his short steps to match the long steps of the old man walking beside him. "It is good to have a secret, Grandpapa."

"Yes," the old man said. "It is good to have a secret if the secret is a good one."

"It is good." Tony smiled shyly. "It will be good for you."

"For me? Is it to be for me?"

"That is my secret. That is my secret," Tony sang as he danced along. Ahead of him now, he could see his little pink house hiding behind the tall green trees. "Tomorrow I will know if I can work for money. Money is important."

"Perhaps." Grandpapa patted Tony's hand. "Perhaps. Anyway, tomorrow we will know. Tomorrow always answers today's questions."

"Not tomorrow, but the day after tomorrow, Grandpapa. Tomorrow will be the day of waiting. It is the next day that I will pick the coffee berries."

"Perhaps," Grandpapa said.

"Perhaps. Perhaps. Perhaps I will have money. Money is important."

Tony sang, and somewhere in a tall tree a songbird answered him, mocking him, singing, too— "Im–por–tant. Im–por–tant."

3. Money Can Buy Things

AT HOME Mama and Maria Rosita had finished washing the clothes. All the things that they had washed
were lying on the grassy ground. They smelled clean
and good. They were very soapy. In two or three days, after the
sun and the rain had made the clothes even cleaner than the soap
and water had made them, Mama and Rosita would gather them.
They would put them in clean water in the cement tub. They
would rinse them. They would put them on the grass to dry again.

Now Maria Rosita was pounding corn to make into tortillas.
Mama ground coffee. When Grandpapa and Tony came in, they
sniffed the sweet corn and coffee smells. Mama was happy to see
them.

"Now that you are here, you must eat with us," she told the old
man. "Soon Papa will be home, and Roberto is here now. He is
swimming in the river to clean himself after the day's work."

As she spoke Papa and his oxen came down the road by the
sugar mill where the brown sugar was boiled into sweet cakes of
dulce. Grandpapa was the first to hear the ox-cart.

"Listen," he said, "there is the Papa now. Can't you hear the
singing ox-cart? It is the Papa's song the ox-cart sings. I can tell.
I know it."

Grandpapa and Rosita, Mama and Tony, went out on the
corredor to wave at Papa and to watch the two great oxen pull
the creaking cart down the muddy road.

Roberto came running from the river. His thick black hair was
plastered to his head like a shining black hood. As always he

laughed and teased his sister. "Rosita, Papa did not sell the pig. It ran away." Roberto spread his hands out. "No pig, no money, no shoes. Ay, ay, our pretty one will have to take her toes bare to San José."

Maria Rosita turned her back to him. This was no time for joking.

The family began calling to Papa as he walked before his oxen, his long ox goad over his shoulder.

"Did you bring it—the money?"

"Is there enough?"

"Do you know? Do the shoes cost a fortune?"

"Too bad the pig ran away. Rosita is not pleased." That was Roberto speaking. Teasing, as always.

"That pig was a good one. It should have sold for a big price." Grandpapa sounded sorry.

"I think he is sad because Papa had to sell the pig," Tony thought, but aloud he said, "Did you bring me something, Papa?"

Papa laughed at them. He waved his long ox goad. He touched the ox yoke gently with it to tell his oxen, "All is well. Keep straight ahead. We are home again."

Tony ran to meet him. He walked with his father in front of the two great oxen. The ox-cart's song was loud. To Tony the song sounded like, "Long way—long way—long way to San José."

Roberto came to unyoke the oxen, to rub them down, to feed them sugar cane, and then to lead them to the field for their night of resting.

Papa went into the house. The others followed him. His market bag was full of things. He took it from his shoulder and began to show what he had brought home.

"This is salt, Mama. You needed it, perhaps?"

"Yes, yes. Did you buy it?"

"No, when I stopped at the resting place with my oxen, men from the salt camp were there. They had just come up from the seacoast and had brought this sea salt with them. I traded the can of shelled peas for it."

"It is not very pure. There is still much sand in it."

"Yes, but that is of little importance since you use so little of it."

"What is this, Papa, lard? I do not need lard. I have enough."

"Well, the hens that I traded for it were thin hens, Mama. You should have sent fat hens to market."

"The pig, Papa, did you sell it?"

Papa took candles from his market bag. "These are for the old one. Maria Rosita's bananas bought them."

Grandpapa took the candles. He looked at them with pleasure. Having candles the nights when his old eyes refused to shut themselves in sleep would not seem so long. They would be bright with a candle's yellow light.

"Ah, what else have I? Soap? It is here. Matches? Yes, I have them."

"Papa, what about the pig? Did you sell it?"

"I told you, pretty sister, the pig ran away."

"Hush, you, Roberto! Stop teasing your sister." Mama stood in front of Roberto. She looked small beside her tall son, but her voice sounded big as she spoke.

"Shoes, Papa?" she asked him. "Did you look at shoes?"

Papa seemed surprised. "Shoes, little Mama? Shoes? The rich wear shoes. Perhaps I saw them. The rich are always at market. They come to buy what we have to sell." Papa looked into his bag again. He kept on talking. "Here," Papa looked around Mama at the laughing Roberto, "here is a new denim apron for you. The old one you are wearing is mine. Now you can give it back to me."

Papa looked again into his market bag. "Oh! Here is red candy for my precious Tony."

"Papa!" Mama stood close to him. "Papa, did you—"

Papa laughed. He spoke quickly, "I almost forgot about the pig. I sold him. Perhaps you forgot that I took the pig to market to sell for money. Well, I sold him. I got money for him. Here it is, Mama. How about getting some shoes for our beautiful daughter to wear to San José?"

Rosita said, "Oh, Papa!"

Roberto said, "That is good."

Grandpapa said, "It was a good pig. Better than shoes, I think."

Mama looked at everyone. She was smiling. Her black eyes shone in the soft lamplight.

"Ay, ay!" she laughed. "Your Papa is a good man."

Tony looked at his red candy. He could count it. There were five big pieces and four small ones. Nine, that made. Nine, one for each of his years, but he was almost ten. Tony emptied the candy bag. Yes, there was a broken bit of candy. A piece of one that made it almost ten. Tony put the candy back into the paper bag again, counting each piece carefully. Candy must be eaten slowly and made to last. Having candy was not a happening of everyday.

"See what Papa bought for me," he told Roberto. "He bought it with money at the market."

"Just as I said," Roberto said. "Money is magic."

"That one must have his joke," Grandpapa grumbled, but Papa was pleased. He was feeling good. He liked Roberto's joking.

Mama called to them to eat the supper she had made ready for them. Everyone was hungry. Everyone ate and talked and laughed. It was a happy time. When supper was finished, the family sat for a while, talking quietly.

The lamplight made gray shadows in the corners of the room. Outside was not quite dark. Twilight was soft and silvery. The birds were twittering among themselves, getting their feathers ready for a night of sleeping and putting their songs to bed.

Grandpapa said, "Tony wants something. He wants something for someone. That is what he tells me. It is something that he has to buy with money that he himself must earn."

Papa said, "So? Money is hard to get."

Grandpapa looked at Mama. "I have told Tony," he said to Mama, "that if his Papa lets him, he can go coffee picking with you on the day that you go—the day after tomorrow."

Mama said, "But coffee picking is hard work."

"That is true," the old man answered, "and being true maybe the Patron will pay him money for his work."

"He is too young," Papa said.

Mama said, "Yes. He is too young."

"But he can try. If he gets money for it—good. If he doesn't, at least we did not think he would."

Papa pushed his lips out. He rubbed his fingers across his chin. "That is true, but—"

Rosita and Roberto spoke. "Let him try," they said together. "Let him try, Papa."

"Yes," Mama said, "Papa will let him. As for me, I am not certain, but Papa will let him do it. Won't you, Papa?"

Papa said, "Well—"

"See! What did I tell you!" Mama said.

Everyone said, "Good. Papa will let him."

Grandpapa went home, down the road to his little pink house. He took the candles with him. He was smiling. It had been a good day.

The night was still and clear. The moon smiled down on the coffee plants and the bananas and the pineapples, crowding so close to Tony's house.

The family went to bed and to sleep. Papa dreamed of a new pig that he could have to keep and not to sell. Rosita dreamed of wearing shoes, beautiful shoes, and of working in Niña Lygia's house in San José.

Tony's dream was the best of all. He dreamed that he had money and, having money—pooff—just as Roberto said, he could buy things. His secret came true. He saw himself and what he had bought walking down the road to his Grandpapa's house. It was a wonderful dream.

Tony smiled in his sleep. He whispered in his dream, "Yes, yes. Money can buy things."

The moon looked in at the window and smiled at the sleeping boy. Outside a night bird cried and then was still.

4. Waiting Is Difficult

THIS morning excitement ran around and around and around in Tony's house.

Mama made everyone get up long before the sun had called the world to waken. Last night's rain was heavy on the velvet leaves of the coffee trees. Everything was wet—the ferns, the vines, and the tall grass. Everything smelled damp. The world outside the house was heavy with its stored-up water. The world outside the house was slow and gray and still and cold.

Inside the house everything was hurry, hurry, hurry. Hurry to wake up, to get up, to dress, to eat. Mama bustled around. Rosita bustled around. Even Papa and Roberto and Tony hurried a little. Mama made them hurry.

Breakfast was scanty and quick this morning. There was no time for making little hills of rice and beans and eating around them and through them, like other mornings.

Rosita was going to San José. She would stay there. She would work in the big house of Niña Lygia, sister of the Patron. This was Rosita's first time away from home. This was the first time that she would stay in the wonderful city, live there, walk its streets, look into its stores, be a part of its everyday life.

More than that! This was the day when Mama would buy Rosita shoes. Oh, blessed Costa Rica! Good, kind country! Its poor could go up, step by step, into the world where the rich people lived. The poor could have shoes, houses, automobiles, anything that they could buy, if they could get the money. This was like that wonderful country called the United States. There were no laws saying that the poor must be poor until they died.

"This is a wonderful country, Papa. Costa Rica is a good, beautiful, wonderful country." Mama put the coffee pot on the table. She stood there, smiling at her family.

Papa looked surprised. He had thought that Mama was excited because Rosita was going to work in San José and because this was the day when Mama would take the money to the city to buy Rosita shoes. Papa felt that sometimes he did not understand the thoughts that Mama had. They went so fast, like Mama's dancing feet when she danced to the music of the marimba. But Papa was happy, Papa was happy that Mama loved their country. He too knew that Costa Rica was a beautiful and good place. He began to answer Mama, but Mama was talking again. This time she said, "I have told her if they hurt, to take them off. She need wear them only on the street."

Papa gave up. He looked at Roberto and Tony, but they were busy. They were eating rice and beans. Mama and Rosita finished their breakfast. Mama helped Rosita pack her dresses and her aprons in the large square basket, the one that had a woven cover.

Papa ate his rice and beans.

Mama and Rosita packed and talked and laughed and packed and talked. Finally the packing was finished. Rosita put on her prettiest apron over her long, ruffled skirt. She put her colored kerchief around her shoulders. She tied ribbons in her two long black braids.

Grandpapa came in the door. He too had wakened early on this important morning. He brought a wire basket of purple orchids for Maria Rosita to take to her new home.

Rosita kissed the old man good-by. She kissed Roberto and Tony and last of all her Papa. "You are a good Papa," she told him.

There were tears in her eyes. Now everyone was crying and laughing, both together. They were crying because their beautiful Rosita was going away from them. They were laughing because she was going to San José, and they knew that she would be happy there.

The big yellow bus came honking down the road by the Patron's sugar mill. "There is the bus, there is the bus," everyone cried as they ran out to wave to it to stop.

The bus was full of people. Men and women hung out of the windows, laughing and waving at everything they saw. Pigs and chickens were tied on the back of the bus. Baskets and sacks were tied on top of the bus.

"There is no space," Rosita cried. "We cannot go. There is no space."

"There is always space. If not to sit, there is space to stand." While Mama talked, she helped the driver put Rosita's basket on top of the bus. She took Rosita's flowers and held them high. She pushed Rosita in ahead of her. She found a place to sit and pushed Rosita into it. She called good-by.

The bus started. Its gears screeched. Its tires screeched. It groaned and rumbled beneath its load. The motor roared. The exhaust pipe puffed. The driver honked and shouted. The pigs squealed and the chickens squawked. The people laughed and shouted. They started. They were off. They had gone.

A dog that had run barking at the big bus wheels came back, his head drooping, his tongue hanging out. He threw himself in the cool long grass to wait for the next bus. He might have better luck next time. His barking might be heard.

For a minute the four who were left behind stood by the road and watched the bus get smaller and smaller. The world was still again. The sun came up. The world woke up, but quietly, now that the hustle and the bustle and the excitement were gone with the bus out of sight and out of sound.

Then Roberto went to the Patron's house to begin his work for the day. Grandpapa and Papa went to yoke the oxen to the ox-cart. Papa had promised the Patron that today he would clean the plantation of all the old, dead coffee trees. He and Grandpapa could use the coffee wood for many things.

Tony was left alone. The house seemed very empty. There was food on the table, but he was not hungry. He could not eat. All he could do was wait for tomorrow. Then his dream would come true.

He sat on the corredor and looked out at his world. The sun was warming the flowers. It was drying the rain on the leaves and the grass.

Tony was thinking about his Grandpapa. "My Grandpapa, the poor one, now that his old ox is dead, he is lonely. I watched him this morning as he helped Papa get his oxen yoked. I watched his hands touch the oxen so gently. I saw his eyes look at Papa's ox-cart. I know what he was thinking. He was thinking of his own beautiful ox-cart with the orchids painted on it. He was thinking how it is, now, with his ox-cart. It is standing on the corredor day after day with nothing to do now that there are no oxen to pull it. Poor Grandpapa!"

A tear slid down Tony's nose and rested on his red little mouth. It tasted salty, just like a tear should taste. To taste his tears made Tony cry some more and then he remembered something. He remembered his secret. The something that he was going to buy for someone comforted him. That beautiful something that he

could buy when he earned the money. That, of course, made him
think about tomorrow.

"You know," Tony told no one because there was no one around
to listen, "you know it might be possible for me to pick more coffee
berries than any one—no, any two men can pick. If that is how it
will be, ay, ay!"

Tony's tears stopped. He was happy again.

Before long Carlos Pedro, José, and Jorge came by. They had
two flat boards nailed together.

"Come on. Play sled with us."

"Sled? Is that a new kind of game? I do not know that game."

José explained. José had been to the United States. He knew
many things, that one, but not all of them were to be believed. His
companions listened eagerly. After they had listened they held the
right to believe or not to believe. Now José told them about the
snow in the United States and about sliding on sleds on its glisten-
ing whiteness.

"This snow," José said, "is very white and very cold and very
deep."

"How white?" Tony asked.

"Very white."

"As white as cotton?"

"Yes, just like cotton."

Now they knew he was not to be believed. They nodded their
heads with satisfaction.

"Cotton isn't cold."

"Well, snow is cold. Colder than the river."

"What's it made of?"

"Water."

"Water? Water isn't white."

José was not pleased with these questions.

"Do you want to play sled or don't you?" he asked them.

They wanted to play. "What do we use for this snow you are telling us about?"

José had an answer for this. He had discovered that the grassy side of a little hill behind the sugar mill was as slick to slide upon as snow.

Playing sled was fun. They took turns sliding down the grassy slippery bank.

"It is as good as snow," José said.

Tony thought it was better because this was real. Grass was real. You could see it. It was here.

When the game grew tiresome, the boys went swimming in the river. They played that there were alligators hiding in the thick ferns along the river bank. They knew there were no alligators here. Farther on, yes, they had seen them, but not here. Here it was safe and therefore fun to play that it was not.

In the late afternoon José sliced a pineapple with his father's long knife that he had brought with him. The boys ate the thick juicy slices of pineapple and told José they hoped his father would not scold him for borrowing his knife.

The river flowed lazily by them as they sat on the grassy bank, chewing sugar cane and talking.

"It will be schooltime again soon," Carlos Pedro said. Carlos Pedro did not like school. He would be glad when he was too old to go any more. Tony was different. Tony liked school. He had gone now for two years and he had learned many things. He had learned to read a little and to write with ink and to count. He had learned many school songs and he had learned to march to music.

"I like school," he told the other boys. "I think our school is a nice place. It has a pretty name."

"Yes," Jorge said. "Flower of the Angels is a good name for a school."

"I will be glad when vacation is over," Tony said.

This reminded José again of how things were in the United

States. "Funny thing about the United States," he said. "Their seasons are turned around up there. They say it is winter when we call it summer here."

"What do you mean?" Carlos Pedro wanted to know.

"Well, December and January and February that are summer with us, they call winter. They have school then. Their school begins in September, not in March as our school does. They have their little vacation in December when we are having our long vacation."

"Is it their rainy season in December?"

"No. They have snow then."

There he was, wanting to talk about snow again.

Carlos Pedro began to speak. He did not want to listen to more talk from José about snow. He said, "I like December to come in summer as it should come. We can have fiestas then because there is no rain."

Jorge nodded his head. "I like Christmas fiesta best. Then there are parades of clowns and funny creatures in the streets of San José."

"Yes. There are bullfights then too."

"My uncle rode a bull once in San José. He did not have a dart or a cape or anything. He just had my aunt's shoulder kerchief to tease the bull before he jumped on his back."

"Did he win a prize?"

"No, he fell off. The bull chased him so he had to jump into the pool of water they have there for just such things."

The boys laughed. It was good to sit here by the river, to eat and to talk and to use the lazy hours that way until day was done.

Jorge talked about the ox-cart parade. He had seen it once when he was very small. That was the year Tony's grandfather had won the prize for the most beautiful painted cart and the best-cared-for oxen.

"That will not happen again," Jorge said, "now that the poor old man has no more oxen."

"It will happen," Tony shouted. "It will happen. Someday my Grandpapa will have new oxen. Big, white, beautiful ones!"

The boys were doubtful. "He is too old to get the money to buy oxen," they said. "What could he do for work? Now that his last ox is dead he cannot haul sugar cane to the sugar mill for the Patron."

"You wait," Tony promised. "You just wait. Someday my Grandpapa will win a prize again. Now I am going home. I almost forgot. Tomorrow I have important work to do."

"You? Important work? What is it?" But Tony did not answer.

Tony went home. He walked quickly. The secret wanting that was in his heart felt big again. It felt like a big lump in his throat.

"Tomorrow, tomorrow, tomorrow," Tony kept saying as he walked along. "Tomorrow is long in coming."

When he reached his little pink house hiding in the trees, his family were waiting for him. It was almost dark. Grandpapa and Papa had a pile of dead coffee-tree wood that Mama could use to burn in her clay stove.

Roberto had finished work too. He was playing his guitar and singing softly.

Mama had come back on the bus. All during supper she told her family about what had happened in San José.

They had bought Rosita's shoes, beautiful ones that had not hurt her feet too much. Then they had gone to Niña Lygia's house. It was a grand house, with many rooms besides the kitchen. It had three courtyards—one for the flowers, one for the washtub and one for the flower garden. Near the garden was the corredor that led to the three little rooms for Niña Lygia's three girls who worked for her. One was the cook. One served Niña Lygia in all her needs. Maria Rosita was the third one. She was to help the cook and the serving maid until she learned how Niña Lygia liked to have things done.

Mama said Rosita's room was pretty. It had a white table and a white chair and a white bed with a blue cover on it. There were blue and white curtains at the window. There was a holy picture on the wall and a vase with crepe-paper flowers on the table. "Just like my vase of flowers," Mama told them.

Once a month, Mama said, Rosita could take the bus and come home for a little visit.

Niña Lygia had sent a long loaf of good crusty bread for the family's supper. Mama had fried a platter full of bananas. Supper tasted good.

The family talked about tomorrow that was now so near in coming.

"Remember you are young, my Tonito," Papa said. "Our Patron pays money only for men's work."

"Tonito can try," Roberto said.

"Yes, you can try, Tonito." Mama's words were kind.

"And anyway," Grandpapa added as he told them good night, "if no money comes, we will not be disappointed, for we did not believe it would be so. We only hoped."

Tony was glad to go to bed and to sleep. The day had been very long. To wait seems harder than anything was his last sleepy thought.

Tony was too tired to dream.

5. Working Is Difficult

"Y ou do it this way," Papa said. He slid his long arm under a branch of the coffee tree. With his other hand he stripped the branch of its cluster of red coffee berries. They poured in a red berry stream into the deep basket Papa wore tied to his waist.

Tony was delighted. "Aren't they pretty, Papa? They look like red raindrops and they sound like raindrops as they fall into the basket. Red rain, Papa, that's what they are."

"Well, the red rainy season is going to be over before you get your share of it, if you do not get started soon," Papa told him.

"Oh, I know how to do it, Papa." Tony had watched the coffee pickers each season for as long as he could remember. It looked easy and quick to do. He watched his father's sure fingers swiftly strip the coffee-tree branch.

"Let me do it," he kept saying. "Let me do it. It is easy."

"It looks easy," his father said. "It looks easy when I do it, little Manuel Antonio. But do not forget, I have done this thing over and over for many more years than you have lived."

Mama came up to where they were. "Help me, Tony," she said. "Put your berries in my basket. You and I, little coffee berry, we will work together."

"I can do my own, Mama, I can do it by myself."

"The small one learns quickly," Papa told her.

"The small one will learn quickly that he has not learned everything," Mama answered. She was not pleased. Manuel Antonio was not acting in the way she thought that he should act.

49

Papa said, "Take this low branch, Tony. Children pick the lower branches."

"I want the high ones, Papa. Remember this is a money-making day for me."

Mama put her hand on her Tony's shoulder. Her eyes told Papa, "Your young son is going to have a bad day. I am sorry for him."

Tony picked up the coffee basket that had been given him. It was almost as tall as he was. He could not see over it. He could not see around it. He could not carry it and walk and hold the tree branch against his arm and strip the little berries all at the same time.

Mama scolded because there were no smaller baskets. She had forgotten that she had offered to share her basket with this little coffee picker. She had forgotten that he had acted naughty.

"These baskets," she scolded. "These baskets are too big for man or ox to carry."

Papa smiled at Tony. "Your Mama would have little baskets and little trees for little boys." He put some of the berries he had picked into Tony's basket.

Mama stood there. She did not know what to do. Tony did not want to let her help him. He did not want to strip just the low branches. He did not want to use some other kind of basket.

"If he must jump over the river before he has learned how to hop the puddles, he is going to get wet," and she shrugged her shoulders. She was sorry for Tony, but what could she do about it if he would not listen? "Well!" Mama shrugged her shoulders again. She smiled at Tony, but she did not wait for him. After all, she had come to pick coffee.

Mama was a good coffee picker. It was her pride always to be the first in line at the weighing cart. It made her proud to bring

home many of the little round tags the manager gave for each full coffee basket. These tags were worth money when the Patron paid them for their work.

Mama went down the row of coffee trees, her big coffee basket tied to her waist. Her brown feet touched the earth lightly. Her brown hand held the coffee tree branch tightly. Her slender brown fingers stripped the coffee branch swiftly of its berries.

Mama sang as she worked. If she remembered the struggling young coffee picker behind her, no one could tell by her song.

Papa was patient. He said, "See, Tony, this is the way to do it. After all, coffee trees are not so high. They almost are made for boys like you."

Papa leaned against a large tree in among the bush-like coffee trees. Tony knew what it was. He knew it was a madroño tree. He knew what its work was. It was there to help the coffee trees. It was there to shade them from the too hot sun. It was there to make life better for them.

The air was alive with song, sweet, golden Costa Rican music.

Then someone's laughter would break the song. One could almost hear its tinkling pieces fall into silence. But soon, again there would be gay calling and happy talking among the coffee trees. Soon a new song would start.

The morning sun shone brightly through the velvet coffee leaves. It left lace patterns of sunlight and shadow where it touched. A breeze came to dry Tony's wet forehead. It whispered through the bushy trees, "I would help you, Tony, if I could."

Tony did not hear it. He did not listen. He was picking coffee berries. It was hard work. Tony was tired.

Someone saw a snake. Someone killed it. The talk and the laughter grew louder to drown the fear.

Papa came back, walking quickly. He looked to see if all was well with Mama's little coffee berry. Tony did not see him. Papa quietly walked away.

The breeze played hide-and-seek through the coffee leaves with the sunlight and the shadows. It fanned the workers to cool them and to help them with their picking.

Coffee-picking time in Costa Rica is the gayest time of the year. The country people from near and far come to work on the coffee plantations. The people like to pick coffee. They like to work together. They like to visit with their neighbors. They like the fun of seeing who first can fill his coffee basket.

Country girls who go to work in the city get lonesome for home at coffee-picking time. The houses of the rich are fairylands to them all through the year—except at coffee-picking season. Then they want to come home to the country. The country calls them. Coffee berries call them.

Shoes hurt and the city streets are hard to walk upon when the winds sing, "Country people are picking coffee and the earth is soft and damp and warm."

Tony wished that today he could look up and see his sister, the beautiful Maria Rosita. He felt lonely for her. He would like to see her slipping quickly between the rows of trees, carrying her coffee basket and singing country people's songs.

He knew that she would not come. Not now. Mama had told him that Maria Rosita had promised. She had promised Niña Lygia that she would stay in San José this coffee-picking season.

Tony wiped two tears away. One tear was for Maria Rosita, because she could not be here this year. One tear was for himself, because picking coffee berries was so much work.

Tony heard something. He looked around. There was Roberto.

"You have finished delivering the milk that you are here where you do not belong?" Tony sounded cross. He wanted to sound that way. No one must know that a few tears had come, uninvited, to stay with him a while.

Roberto laughed. "Well, yes," he answered his young brother. "I hurried with the milk. I thought they might need my help for a few hours." Roberto laughed again. Quickly he stripped a branch of berries into Tony's basket.

Tony looked into his basket. He gave a little half-laugh. "Well! I cannot see the bottom any more. At least the bottom of my basket is covered with berries."

When he looked up again, Roberto was gone. Then he heard him talking. Tony peeked around a tall madroño tree.

Aha! Roberto was talking to that pretty Teresita. He was teasing her, that pretty one who lived two pink houses from Grandpapa's house.

Aha! Maybe Roberto was Teresita's sweetheart. Tony had not thought of his big brother as being some girl's sweetheart. He had not thought of that before. He would watch next time the family went to San Ramón. He, Tony, would watch the grand march. That was something to watch anyway.

All the small boys liked to watch the grand march, when the young girls walked one way around the village park and the young men walked the other way.

Tony sat down. "This coffee basket needs resting, I think," he said to himself.

While he was sitting down he thought some more about the grand march and Teresita and Roberto. If they looked at each other and smiled as they passed in the walking circles, then Tony would know. He would know without the shadow of a doubt. If they smiled at each other, Roberto would be Teresita's sweetheart!

It must be wonderful to be old enough to be some pretty girl's sweetheart. Tony sighed. It must be wonderful to have some pretty girl think you were dashing and handsome. Tony yawned. He rested his head against the coffee basket. His long, black lashes lay tight against his rosy cheeks. His head nodded.

Coffee picking went on, with its swiftly moving people and their Costa Rican songs and laughter. By a coffee tree and a coffee basket a very young coffee picker slept. Picking coffee berries is hard work for one who is not quite ten years old.

6. Money Must Be Earned

TONY, Tony, wake up! Wake up!" Mama was calling, calling to her sleeping boy.

"Wake up, Tony. Something nice is going to happen for you and for all of us." Papa was gently shaking his sleeping boy.

Tony's black eyes opened. "Where is my basket? Where is my coffee basket?"

"The manager took it. He weighed it in with mine," Papa answered. "You helped me get my basket full."

Tony said, "I wanted to fill it myself. Do you suppose I slept a little?"

Papa laughed. "A little, I think."

Mama laughed too. "You slept all the hours of midday. You slept while everyone else was picking."

"But," Papa added quickly before Tony had time to feel bad about sleeping, "but you wakened just in time for the party."

"Party, Papa? Party?"

"Yes, yes. Our good Patron." Mama's words were quick and fast. They were always quick and fast when she was pleased. "Our good Patron is giving us a picnic fiesta. Can't you smell the coffee?"

"Can't you smell the candy cooking, sleepy one?" called Roberto as he came hurrying down the coffee-tree row.

"Candy?" Tony was very wide-awake. His nose sniffed the rich sweet smell of boiling taffy. Sobado, Costa Ricans call it. It is their favorite candy. They always have it at fiestas.

Tony stood up. He shouted, "Come on!" He and Mama hurried to the outdoor coffee-drying floors where the party already had begun. Papa and Roberto hurried after them, but even their long legs could not keep up with Mama's flying feet.

The flat cement of the drying floors felt hot on Tony's feet as he ran down the wide stair-like floors. He hopped across the steep, narrow cement ditches. There was no water running in them now. After the coffee beans are sorted and cleaned, then the water carries them to the different drying floors. But now the ditches were dry. The coffee-drying floors were bare of coffee.

The pickers were there instead. Some were drinking coffee. Some were pulling taffy. Others were dancing to the gay music of the plantation band.

"Why do we have fiesta now?" Tony asked. "This is only the first day of picking, not the last day."

"I do not know," Mama answered. "Perhaps the Patron is happy about something. It seems that way."

Now that there was a party, other children of Tony's age had come to the drying floors. No one stopped to ask them how they knew about the party or how they came so quickly. It was enough that they were there. Parties are nicer when all the family can be a part of them. Tony's friends were with him now, but he was the youngest coffee picker. All the grownups came over to speak to him.

"You work well." "Fine." "Good." "Yes, you work well." "Before too long you may be as good a picker as your Papa," they said.

No one told them that this young picker had spent most of the picking time asleep beside his coffee basket. At first Tony was afraid that someone would tell about his nap.

He looked at his family. They were smiling and nodding their

heads at all the wonderful things the people were saying to Tony. They looked as if they believed what the people were saying.

After a time Tony forgot about his nap. He believed what they were saying too. He answered, "Yes, thank you." "Thank you, Señor." "Yes, Señora, I expect I will be as good a picker as my Papa."

"Someday, maybe." Tony looked around to see who said those words.

It was Roberto! He had said them. Tony was not pleased. He remembered what his Grandpapa had said about Roberto. So now he repeated it. He told the people who were standing near him, "That one always has to have his joke."

The people laughed. Roberto laughed too. He gave his younger brother a little spank. Then he went away to ask Teresita's Mama if Teresita could dance with him.

Mama gave Tony another piece of candy.

Soon the Patron himself came by. "I hear I have a new coffee picker on my plantation," he said gravely to Tony. "Which one is this one?" he asked.

"My son," Papa told him.

"My son, Manuel Antonio," Mama told him.

"I am Tony," Tony said as he put out his hand for the Patron to shake.

The Patron shook Tony's hand. Then he laughed. His laugh was big and deep. "Well, picker," he told the little boy. "I have a present for you. Come, I will give you coffee to take home, and candy too. My pickers must be well paid for the coffee they pick."

"I did not pick much, Don Ramón," Tony told him. He hated to say it, but, after all, he had not picked very many berries. He had slept. To be honest was even more important than to make money.

"I know," the Patron answered. "I know. This that I am giving you is really a gift, not pay."

Tony was happy. He went with the Patron to get his bag of candy and his bag of coffee. He walked with the Patron across the drying floors. He and the Patron walked together, as men do, for all the world to see.

When he came back, Mama said that the party was over. They must go home. Tony and Mama and Papa walked home. Roberto was not with them.

"Where is your other son?" Tony asked his father. "Why does he not walk with us?"

Papa laughed, and Mama said, "I am glad that you slept this afternoon."

Tony looked at her. That Mama! Now he felt like a small boy again. He did not feel like the right-hand man of the Patron.

Papa took Tony's hand. He said, "Mama is a beautiful woman." Somehow that made things right again. It was as if Papa had said, "My son, we understand Mama, do we not?"

They walked along the narrow ribbon of road that went winding among the trees and led to home. Soon they saw their little pink house. Lamplight was shining through the windows. Someone was there. Someone was waiting for them to come home.

It was Grandpapa. He was sitting in the chair by the window.

Suddenly Tony remembered about wanting to pick coffee for money. He remembered that he wanted to earn money to buy something for someone. He had slept. He had not picked a basketful of coffee berries. He had no money. He had not earned it. He had only a gift of candy and coffee.

He went to stand shyly beside Grandpapa's chair.

"My Grandpapa, I went to sleep. I did not earn the money that

I wanted. Here is a present for you, Grandpapa, coffee and candy."

"Is this what you earned for the berries you picked before sleep played that trick on you?"

"No, Grandpapa, I did not earn anything. The Patron gave them to me as a gift, and I share them with you."

Mama and Papa hurried to tell Grandpapa all the nice things that had happened during the day. They told about the fiesta. They told what the Patron had said to Tony. They did not want their Tonito to feel badly. They thought that talk would help.

By and by Roberto came home. He was very happy and very gay and very pleased with everything. He played his guitar and Papa helped him sing. Mama made coffee. Grandpapa passed the candy around and around.

"We are having our own fiesta," Mama said. Everyone said, "Yes. This is a wonderful party." Everyone but Tony.

Tony was quiet. Tony had sad thoughts now that he remembered about his secret, sad thoughts because he had slept and had not earned money. "Poor Grandpapa," he said to himself. "I must get money to buy that secret that I want to buy."

Grandpapa kept looking at his young grandson. Even when he was being very gay with Papa and Roberto, he kept looking at Tony. "I wonder what he wants so much," he thought. "Whatever it is, I wish I could help him get it."

Papa said to the old man, "Stay the night with us. Sleep here."

Grandpapa shook his head. "No," he said. "No. I have been thinking. Now that my last ox is dead there is no work for me, but perhaps—" Grandpapa stopped to think some more about what he was saying.

"Yes. Tomorrow I will take our Manuel Antonio to the sugar mill where I worked before my oxen died. There might be something he could do there. Knowing me, it might help if I took him."

Papa said, "He is too young." But Mama said that he should try. "It is part of growing up to be a man," she told them. "This one will not grow up the easy way. He can learn to stumble proudly." Mama got up to look out into the night. She was quiet for a minute. When she turned back she said, "We can always have a party afterward."

Papa nodded. So did Roberto and Grandpapa. Tony did not understand their words, but he knew that it was all right. That tomorrow he could try again.

Grandpapa stood up. "Let Tony come home to sleep with me tonight. We will waken early in the morning."

Mama said, "Yes."

Tony was happy again. Happy because he could spend the night at Grandpapa's house, and happy because once again his dream was almost coming true.

Grandpapa and Tony walked down the road. Grandpapa's lantern made a white light for them to walk into. They did not talk. They walked quietly so as not to waken the sleeping world.

To stay with Grandpapa was an honor. It was an honor that did not happen every day. It did not happen to everybody. Even to Tony it did not happen often.

"It makes me happy to stay with you, Grandpapa," Tony said and gave a little skip. He put his small hand shyly into his grand-father's large one. It was good to hold his grandfather's hand. Just for tonight he was glad he did not have to be a man. "It is wonderful to stay in your house, Grandpapa. Your house is better to stay in than—" Tony thought a minute—"better than staying at the Patron's house."

Grandpapa laughed at this and Tony laughed too. What a thing to say! To even think! Staying at the Patron's house! As if he ever could!

They walked along in silence. Underneath their feet the ground felt damp and cool. The velvet night lay soft around them. There were no noises except those sleepy sounds, almost like shadows, that fill the wooded places when night has come.

Soon they reached Grandpapa's house. It did not look pink in the night's gray light. It looked gray like the world around it. The ox-cart on the corredor looked big and black. Even at night it looked lonely.

They went inside. Grandpapa got the candles down from the peg on the wall where they were hanging.

Grandpapa lighted a candle. He carefully hung the others up again. Tony looked at them. Only one had been used, and only a little. A lump came into his throat. Even candles were precious to Grandpapa now that he could not work.

Grandpapa put the mats on the hard board beds. He brought a blanket from his basket for Tony's bed.

Did Grandpapa have a blanket too? Tony wondered. He looked through his long thick eyelashes. He looked quickly at Grandpapa's bed. It would not do for Grandpapa to see him looking. He would not like it. But yes, it was all right. Tony saw that Grandpapa had a blanket too. Grandpapa blew out the candle flame. For a little time the wick was a glowing stem. Tony watched it. Then it became a part of the darkness.

Soon they were in their beds, the tired old man and the tired young boy. It had been a long day for both of them. Tony did not know it, but his wanting something for someone so badly hurt the old man deeply. To think that a grandson of his should need money to buy a thing of happiness, and he, the grandfather of the small one, did not have money to give him. Ah! It was a knife in the heart!

The old man tossed on his mat bed.

"Grandpapa," Tony was not asleep. "Do you think that tomorrow will bring me money for my secret? You know, to work at the sugar mill?"

"Perhaps, if the good God wills it."

"Grandpapa, I need to tell you something. Do you know that nine-year-old boys need help with working? If they try to do it all alone, they might go to sleep."

"Yes, Tonito, I know. I am glad you know it too."

"I did not know it until today, Grandpapa. Tomorrow, at the sugar mill, will you help me, please?"

"Yes, Tonito, I will help you."

Tony tried to say thank you. He tried to say good night but long before he could get them said, he was asleep.

Grandpapa was sleeping too. At last the long, long day had ended for both of them.

7. Work Must Be Learned

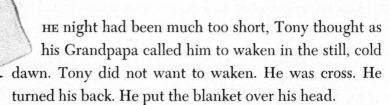

THE night had been much too short, Tony thought as his Grandpapa called him to waken in the still, cold dawn. Tony did not want to waken. He was cross. He turned his back. He put the blanket over his head.

Grandpapa said, "All right, sleepy one. That sugar mill can wait for us to come another day."

Tony rolled over and rolled out of bed. "I'm awake. See me, Grandpapa, see how awake I am!"

Grandpapa had breakfast on the table. Good strong coffee with milk and brown sugar, corn tortillas and white cheese.

"Oh, oh, I like this," Tony sang as he spread the white cheese thick on his tortilla. "We do not have this at our house. I do not know what Mama does with all the milk Roberto brings her. She does not make cheese like this with it."

"Your Mama gave this cheese to me. She brings some to me every day."

Tony did not know what to say. He hoped Grandpapa did not guess how the milk Roberto brought had been used.

"This coffee burns my mouth," he said just to have something new to talk about.

Grandpapa looked surprised. The coffee was not very hot. "So," he said, drawing it out, making it a long word, "so–oo."

66

Tony laughed. "That was teasing," he said. He was pleased with himself for having thought so quickly of a way to change the conversation.

Grandpapa looked surprised again. He asked, "Teasing? Was that teasing?" But he laughed. It was good to have someone at his breakfast table.

After breakfast Grandpapa put his house in order. Then he made tortilla sandwiches filled with mashed bean paste. He wrapped them in banana leaves. He put coffee in a tin pail and gave Tony a hollow gourd for a drinking cup. This was for their midday lunch. Then they were ready to go.

As they walked across the corredor into the morning, the sun filled the world with sunrise colors.

"Old Volcan wears a bright scarf this morning, Grandpapa," Tony said, pointing to the bright clouds across the top of the volcano, which did look like a gay kerchief across its shoulders.

The morning was filled with bird song and flower perfume. All the world was busy saying good morning to the bright new day. A leafless tree by the river bank had dressed itself in purple flowers. There were no leaves on its bare branches, but it was bursting with bloom. Later there would be many such trees. This one was a little early. It amused Tony. He called laughingly to his Grandpapa, "Look! That tree is in such a hurry to be beautiful it cannot wait for its leaves to come."

Far up the road an ox-cart could be heard. The old man listened. Then he said, "That cart belongs to José Miguel."

"How do you know? We cannot see it. It is too far away."

"You ask me how I know? I hear the ox-cart's song. That's how I know. Can't you hear the ox-cart singing? Don't you know, Manuel Antonio, that each ox-cart sings the song of its owner? Do you not know that Costa Rica is famous for its singing ox-carts?"

"Yes, I know about our ox-carts singing. I know why they sing too. It is because of the way the wheels are fitted to the axle."

"So–oo!"

"But, Grandpapa, I cannot tell whose cart it is just by the song."

"You will. You will learn. I can. As far away as I can hear an ox-cart I can name its owner."

The ox-cart was in sight now. It was true. José Miguel was walking before his oxen.

"*Adios,*" Grandpapa and Tony greeted him.

"*Adios,*" José Miguel answered in the Costa Rican way.

"Grandpapa, you are a wonderful man. You were right about that ox-cart. You are really wonderful."

This was the time for Grandpapa to change the conversation. "Look! Old Volcan is busy this morning."

Tony looked at the volcano. It did look as if smoke was coming from its cup-like top. But it could be clouds. It could be steam. Some other time he would ask Grandpapa to tell him about the many volcanic eruptions he had seen and the many earthquakes he had been in. But not now. Not this morning.

This morning Tony wanted to talk about work at the sugar mill. This might be the day when he earned money. With money in his hand, his dream-come-true was as close as around the bend of the road.

Tony wanted to tell Grandpapa what his secret was. But no! He must not do it. "That would be wanting him to praise me for what I am going to do," Tony thought. "No, it is the something itself that is important, not just my wanting to do it. I must wait until I have the money. Then I will ask him to go with me to help me in the buying."

Aloud Tony said, "My secret feels like a butterfly in my mouth. Someday it will fly out and you will know what it is."

"When it flies out, that will be good. It will mean that its wings are ready for flying. It will be time for me to know."

Tony puffed his cheeks out and pushed his lips out and squinted his eyes. "Grandpapa, look at me. I am talking with my mouth full of butterflies."

"Better not swallow any," Grandpapa told him gravely.

Tony laughed. Grandpapa was fun. He could play pretend like any boy.

The sugar mill was just ahead of them. It had no walls, just corners and a sloping red-tile roof. Honeysuckle vines stretched their perfumed fingers over the mossy tiles and covered the sloping roof with tangled flowers. At one side was the powerful waterwheel that turned, and turned, and turned the rollers to crush the sugar cane to sweet thick juice.

Everyone was happy to see the old man. They crowded around him, talking and laughing. He had worked with most of them for many seasons. When he was young he had been a cutter in the sugar-cane fields. For the last few years he had used his oxen to pull the heavy cartloads of sugar-cane stalks from the field to the mill.

"Who brings the loaded cart in my place?" the old man asked slowly.

"Oh, that one, Tomas," they answered just as slowly. Grandpapa did not say, "I am sorry it is not I who drive the oxen." No one said, "We are sorry you are not with us." These words were not spoken, but Tony felt them being said in the hearts of the workers.

Two men stood at the waterwheel crusher. One man fed sweet round stalks of sugar cane into the rollers. The man at the other

side pulled out the flattened, broken stalks that the rollers had crushed. With a single motion he pulled out each stalk and tossed it high on the pile in back of him. The juice from the crushed sugar cane slowly trickled into the cement vat waiting for it.

"Perhaps I could do that," Tony whispered. "I could feed the cane into the rollers or pull it out when it is crushed."

Grandpapa shook his head. "That is heavy work. See their powerful muscles. See the sweat running in little streams down their bare, strong shoulders. That is heavy work. It would take years of doing, before you could be strong enough for that."

Tony moved over to the second vat. A cane-stalk fire made the sugar juice boil. A man stood there with a wooden paddle, stirring the thick juice so it would not burn. The man watched the boiling juice carefully. He never looked around. He just stood there with his paddle, stirring the thick juice, letting it boil, letting it bubble, stirring it again, so it would cook, but would not burn.

"Could I do that, Grandpapa, do you think?"

Grandpapa shook his head again. "That kind of work takes seasons of doing. A man must learn how hard the juice must be boiled, and how long. See how he watches the bubbles forming? See how he watches it so it will not burn? No, you do not know enough for that."

By the next vat two more men were standing. They wore no shirts. Their trouser legs were rolled up to their knees. Their bare feet were planted firmly on the ground. They too had wooden paddles. They were stirring the thickened juice fast, fast and faster.

"If they do not stir it long enough, it will not harden. If they stir it too long, it will crumble when they put it in the molds."

"Well, maybe I am big enough for that work," Tony said, "or for this work." He had stopped at the last large vat where a young man was dipping up the sugar juice syrup into the sugar-cake molds. These molds were put, row after row, on a low cement table so that the juice inside would harden. After that the sugar cakes were taken from the molds and stacked into piles.

"Just like the wood in Papa's woodpile," Tony laughed.

Bees droned in and out of the sugar mill. They flew about the sugar cakes cooling in the molds. They feasted on the stacked up cool ones. They were so filled with sugar they could scarcely fly. They flew in slow, slow circles over the pile of sugar cakes. Their buzzing was low and slow and sugar-filled.

In the mill there was a kind of patterned movement. Each worker had his own way of bending over, turning to the right, turning to the left, bending over again, repeating and repeating the same motions over and over and over.

The mill was filled with a hot, sweet, thick sugar smell and the lighter, sweeter perfume of honeysuckle flowers.

The mill was filled with soft, slow, thickened sound. The gurgling of the water, the creaking of the waterwheel, the dripping of the juice, the boiling of the sugar syrup, the spanking sound of wooden paddles, and the lazy droning of the sugar-filled bees.

Everyone was eating broken bits of warm brown sugar. Tony felt sleepy. Movements and smells and sounds and tastes ran together, like a lullaby singing him to sleep. He yawned. He stretched. He made his eyes stay open. He must not go to sleep. To sleep today would be a terrible thing! He must walk. He must get outside where the air was cool and wide-awake.

Finally he said, "Grandpapa, please take me to the cane field. Show me how you cut the sugar cane when you were young. Papa always says that you were the best cane-cutter in the cane fields."

"I will take you there this afternoon."

Just then Juan, the manager of the Patron's mill, came in. It was his work to see that dulce-making was done in the right way and that it did not take too long.

Now he was not pleased. "Get these bees out of the dulce," he shouted.

"But, Señor, they fly in. We cannot stop them."

"You can stop them from getting into the sugar molds. Get a boy to shoo them off." He turned away. Then he saw Grandpapa. He walked over to talk to the old man.

"We miss you. How are you? Who is this one with you?" Juan was like that, always stringing his questions together like a chain.

Grandpapa answered, "Yes. I am well. Thank you. This one is the son of my daughter. He is Manuel Antonio."

Tony was proud of Grandpapa. He could string his answers into even a longer chain.

"Good. Fine. Wonderful. He can work this afternoon. Your Manuel Antonio can shoo the bees off the sugar molds. I am tired of bees in my sugar. What do they call you, Manuel Antonio?"

Tony gasped. Now was the time for him to string some answers back to this Juan who could say so much in such a short time. Tony took a deep breath. Then he said, "Tony," and stopped. He could think of nothing more to say.

"Tony. All right, Tony. You have a job for this afternoon. Not even one bee in the sugar mold, mind you!"

Juan turned away, shouting for Alberto to bring the hand cart to take the dulce to the warehouse.

José Miguel came in with his ox-cart piled high with cane stalks. Grandpapa went to talk with him. Tony fed the tired oxen. He thought about his job for the afternoon. It was not a big job. It was just his size. He could do it.

The hacienda bell rang for the noon rest time and the men stopped their work. They sat near the cement vats and unwrapped their tortilla sandwiches from their banana leaves. "*Galletos*," they called them—"little roosters." Tony ate his "little rooster" and drank sweetened coffee from the gourd his Grandpapa had given him.

He was happy.

8. Money Is Not Everything

AFTER lunch the men sat smoking. A few of the younger ones slept, for this was the siesta hour when workers rested.

"If we hurry," Grandpapa said to Tony, "we can go to the cane field and return before the hacienda bell rings the men back to work again."

"Can you show me how you did it when you were young and cut the sugar cane, Grandpapa?"

"Yes, if we hurry."

"We will hurry. We will hurry fast."

Tony and his Grandpapa went out into the hot midday sun. They walked fast. It was not so very far to the cane field and so it did not take them long. The old man's breath came pantingly, but Tony did not notice. He was talking. He was asking questions about sugar-cane cutting. He was impatient for his Grandpapa to show how good he once had been.

At the cane field the workers were resting. They were taking their siesta in the shadows of the tall sugar cane. But now that Grandpapa had come among them, they crowded around him. They too wanted to see him cut cane.

Some of the older ones had watched him, years ago, when he had been a champion cane-cutter. The younger ones wanted to see him now. They wanted to see if this old man was really good.

No one noticed that the old one was tired from his hurried walking in the midday sun. No one noticed that it was hard for him to breathe. They had forgotten that he was old.

Grandpapa took his long machete where it hung from his belt. He took it in his right hand. He looked at Tony. His eyes were twinkling. They seemed to say, "Aha, Grandson, we will show them what cane-cutting is when a skilled man does it."

Tony smiled back at him, but his smile was impatient. It said, "Hurry, Grandpapa, show them. Show me. Then I must get back. Remember I'm a man of work now back there at the sugar mill."

With his left hand Grandpapa grasped the cane stalk high above his head and slashed it with the sharp machete. He cut off the tough leaves growing around the stalk. Then he bent the cane stalk and let it snap back against his machete blade. He tossed the pieces in a pile.

Grandpapa looked around. He put his hands out, palms up, to say, "Nothing to it, young men, when a skilled man does it!"

The watchers were delighted. It was done so quickly. It had been such sure cutting. It had been so perfect. Grandpapa had not made a gesture or a motion or a movement that was not needed.

"Bravo! Beautiful! Do it again!"

"Do it again! Do it again!" the cutters shouted.

"Oh, Grandpapa, please." Tony's eyes were shining. He felt proud. "Do it again, Grandpapa, again!"

The old man made a little bow to Tony. "For you, Tonito, to remember." Again he cut the cane stalks. Again and again and once again. The pile of cane leaves grew waist-high, and knee-high was the pile of cane stalks.

"Do it again, again!"

The world turned black for the old cane-cutter. The speed of

his young days had been much too fast for his old tired heart. He lay where he had fallen in the cane leaves. The young men ran for cool river water. They watched young Tony kneel beside his grandfather, gently bathing the worn, wrinkled face. Tony did not cry. His eyes felt dry and wide. His heart was cold.

"Grandpapa, my Grandpapa, speak to me."

The men were silent, watching. The old one lay still.

"Grandpapa, Grandpapa."

Far away the hacienda bell rang clearly. Siesta was over. The men turned away to take slow steps toward the work which was waiting. The men turned back again to look down at the quiet old man.

"Grandpapa, speak to me."

The old one opened his eyes. Somehow he sat up. He stood up. He smiled a shaky smile at the worried watchers.

"I must be getting old," he told them. "Come, my Tonito, help me to get home."

The blessed sun hid its burning face behind a cloud. A spatter of rain came to cool the midday air.

Tony and Grandpapa walked slowly. They sat to rest and walked again.

The afternoon was half gone when they reached Grandpapa's clean little house. Tony helped his grandfather lie on the mat on his bed. He made strong coffee for him to drink. Grandpapa slept. Tony sat quietly beside his bed.

Evening came with its lengthening shadows. A night wind whispered its evening song.

Mama and Papa came. Someone had told them what had happened. Mama cooked a big supper. She had been frightened when word had come that the old one was ill. She had been frightened

but not too frightened to fill Papa's market bag with food from her cupboard.

Now she cooked and scolded. It helped her to scold. Somehow it made the band around her heart not feel so tight. Papa understood. He knew she was not cross.

"Food is what the old one needs," Mama said. "Make him come to live at our house, Papa."

Papa shook his head. He said softly, "No, Mama. The food of

pride is more strengthening to the heart than beans in the mouth."

Mama nodded. Papa was right. He was always right. "You are a good man," she told him.

Grandpapa wakened. He smiled at Mama. "I smell good food," he told her. Then he looked at Tony still sitting quietly by his bed. "I will get up, Tonito. Your Papa will need you and me to help him eat the feast your Mama has cooked for us."

The old man got up. He needed help, a little, but he walked straight. He sat straight too, in his chair at the supper table. The Grandpapa had pride.

Supper was a quiet meal. No one felt like talking. Soon it was over.

Mama and Papa went home. Tony was to stay again at Grandpapa's house.

In the early dark the young boy and the old man sat on the wide, cool corredor and listened to the evening sounds.

"I am sorry about today, Grandson. I am sorry about getting sick. You came home with me. You did not stay to earn the money that you want so badly."

"Money!" Tony shrugged his young shoulders. He held his hands out, palms upward. "Money, my Grandfather? Money is not everything."

The old man was deeply touched and deeply pleased. "Whatever it is that you want, little Tony, must be good. It is teaching you so many things. Money is important. Money must be earned, and today the great lesson, money is not everything."

The moon touched the trees with silver and the night was still.

9. Tony Is Not Happy

RANDPAPA was all rested again. He felt fine. He said he did.

Mama and Papa went to see him. They went to ask him to come home with them. Grandpapa said he was well. He said he felt fine. He felt wonderful. "Why should I go home with you? It is kind of you, but my home is my castle." Grandpapa laughed. He touched his daughter's shoulder lightly. "You are very like your Mama was," he told her gently. "You are beautiful and good."

Mama began to cry a little. Papa walked around. He opened the door. Then he shut it again. Mama said, "We want you with us. We want to take care of you." Papa said yes to all of Mama's words. Papa said, "Besides, we need you in our house. Tell him about our little Tony, Mama."

Grandpapa stood up. He put his old hands on the chair. He held to it tightly. "Tony? What is the matter with our Tony?"

Papa said, "We do not know. He sits on the corredor, thinking about something. He does not go to play with the other boys."

"Yes," Mama added, "he does not play. He does not sing any more. He does not eat so much nor like his food as it has been his way."

"When I wanted him to come with me to walk before my oxen, he said he did not want to go."

"When Maria Rosita sent honey to us from Niña Lygia's house, Tony did not eat his share. Then I made the good cheese, and you know how he likes it. Tony eats so little. It hurts my heart."

"Is he sick? Does he have the chills and fever that sicken so many of our children?"

"No. He is not sick."

"No. He is not sick. His body is as strong as ever."

Grandpapa sat down again. "It is perhaps that he is not happy?"

"He is not happy. We do not know what makes his heart so sad."

Grandpapa put his hand over his eyes. "I know the trouble. It is the secret that he talks about. It is the something that he wants to buy for someone. He is so precious to me, this grandson of mine, and I have no money to give him for what he wants to buy."

"Yes. That is what Roberto tells us. That is what my older son says is grieving the little one." Papa walked to the door again.

"But, no. Do not feel badly about the money," Mama comforted these two men who were so dear to her. "Our Roberto has a free heart. He offered to give Tony his pay. Tony told him no. Tony said that he himself must earn it."

Grandpapa said "So–oo." The old man stood up. He seemed stronger. He seemed younger. "You need me at your house. I can see it. I will go with you for tomorrow. We will talk it over with our small one. Everything will be right again."

Papa stopped walking up and down the room. Mama stood up. She had been sitting on the hard plank bed. Grandpapa pushed his chair against the wall. He looked around his house. Everything was clean. Everything was in order. He told them, "I am ready."

The three went out the door and walked along the road. Papa

held his lantern low so they could see. Mama was laughing now. Everything would soon be right again.

"Where is Tony tonight?" Grandpapa wanted to know.

"Roberto took him to the serenado at the Patron's house."

"So—oo, a serenado. That should make him happy. Whom are they serenading? For whom do the young men sing at the Patron's house?"

"His niece Annabella, who goes to school in the United States."

"Ah! She would get nothing so fine there I can tell you. To hear our young men sing is worth a journey."

Grandpapa began to sing and Papa joined him. Their deep voices played with the golden words of Costa Rican songs, tossing them gaily into the velvet night.

Soon another voice came out to meet them. It was Roberto singing their song with them as he sat on the corredor with his guitar.

"Where is Tony?" Mama called to him as the three came to Papa's house.

"What happened to the serenado?" Grandpapa asked.

"Yes, what happened to it?" Papa added. "Do not tell me that the young men ran out of songs so early in the evening."

Roberto laughed, but his laughter seemed a little sad. "Our Tony could not lift his heart with singing tonight. So we came home."

The family went into the house. Papa lit the lamp and Mama warmed the coffee and heated the milk to go in it.

Soon the family were sitting at the table drinking Mama's good strong coffee. Roberto untied a little package. In it were cookies and cakes from the Patron's serenado.

Grandpapa said, "Tony, it is not like you to be unhappy. You are bringing sadness to this house. Come. Tell us what troubles you. We are here to help you."

Tony spilled a little coffee. He wiped it with his hand. He kept looking down, not up, as was his usual way.

Mama said softly, "Manuel Antonio, perhaps you did not hear. This is your Grandpapa speaking."

Tony looked up. His black eyes were filled with tears. They clung in tiny raindrops to his long thick lashes.

"There is something I must do. I do not want to tell you what it is. It is good and it is needed. I must get it."

Tony ran to stand beside Mama. When a boy is not quite ten years old he can cry a little sometimes.

"If I had the wonderful money, pooff"—Tony snapped his fingers as he had seen Roberto do—"pooff, just like that, I could buy it."

Tony looked at all of them. He was not crying now. After all he really was a big boy except for a short time now and then.

"If it is not I who gets this wonderful money, then it cannot be I who buys the gift I want to buy."

Grandpapa said, "I see how it is with you."

Papa said, "We understand, my son."

Roberto said, "Well, let us talk it over. Surely there is some way that we can help you."

"We are your family, Tony," Mama said softly.

Roberto was talking again. Now he was saying, "We will talk this thing over. You cannot work. You are not old enough. Even for young men work is hard and money is slow in coming."

The family nodded their heads, but no one spoke. They were thinking. Roberto said, "The way it comes to me is this. There is really only one way of getting money. You must have something to sell for it. You sell what you can do or you sell what you have that someone wants."

Mama and Papa said, "Yes, that is the way it is."

Grandpapa looked at Roberto. He was very pleased. "Our Roberto has a head on his shoulders. That one can think," he told the others.

Roberto smiled at him, but he kept talking. "Tony is too young yet to sell what he can do. So he must sell something he has. I myself have a guitar. It would bring money for you, Tony."

Tony shook his head. "No! Not the guitar, Roberto."

Papa said, "I have a new scabbard for my machete. My other one is very worn, but I could make it do, I think. Tony can sell the new one."

Tony shook his head. "No! Not the scabbard, Papa."

Mama ran over to a little box that she kept high on a shelf. "Here are my earrings, Manuel Antonio. They are yours to sell. I wear them so little. Only on the days of fiesta."

Tony said, "No, Mama, no. Not your earrings. What I sell must belong to me."

Mama said, "But what have you, Tony?"

Papa said, "You are young to have possessions. When you are older, but not now, Tony."

Roberto said, "It must be something someone else wants."

Grandpapa had not been talking. He had been thinking. Now he held up his hand for all to be still, for all to listen. "He must make something," he said slowly. "He must make something."

"Yes! Yes! Yes!"

"That is a wonderful plan."

"Will you help me, Grandpapa?"

"Yes."

"But what? What will it be?"

"What will he make?"

"It must be something someone will want to buy."

Grandpapa said, "Quiet. Everyone talks too much. Tomorrow I am going back to my little house. There I can think. Words will not be running my thoughts out of the door."

Tony looked at Grandpapa. His eyes were asking something. Grandpapa answered his question, although it had not been spoken. "Yes, yes, you can go home with me. We will think what to make. Then we will make it. Does this family never go to bed?"

It was good to hear Grandpapa talk that way again. It was a good sign. It was a sign that he was well.

Roberto said, "I am going back to the serenado. They will be missing my fine voice."

"You will be missing the fun, you mean," Mama gave her older son a little pat. "But go along. Young men are young men only once."

"Is that what you say?" Grandpapa said. "I have a mind to go help with the singing myself."

The old man began to sing. As always his rich voice rolled out in golden tones. Papa and Roberto joined in the song. Soon Tony too was singing with them. His clear young voice sounded like a silver bell tinkling high above the deep golden notes of the older men.

Mama laughed. "Stop it! Stop it! You will frighten the birds from the trees." But Mama was not cross. She was happy. She listened to the song of the men of her family and knew that all was well with them again.

Happiness had come to live with them once more.

10. Grandpapa's Promise Comes True

GRANDPAPA did not forget what he had said the night before. He spent the day at Mama's house. He joked and laughed with Mama. He teased Roberto about last night's serenado. He made Roberto tell again and again about all that had happened.

"What men were there?" And when Roberto named the young men who had been in the singing group, Grandpapa nodded his head. "Ah, that one, the son of old Miguel." And after calling off another name, "Half-grown is he now? Why, I remember Santiago when he was but so high." Grandpapa held up his hand, in the way Costa Ricans do to show how tall a person is.

"Where did you stand when you serenaded the young lady of the house?"

"Near the steps leading from the long corredor. Near the windows where we could see them dancing. It was a beautiful thing to see. Electric lights and lovely girls. Ay! Ay! Ay!" Roberto raised his shoulders and his hands and his eyes. He was teasing Grandpapa. Tony could see it. He wished they would not talk so much about the serenado. He wished Grandpapa would talk to him, would tell him what the something-to-make was going to be.

Grandpapa winked at Tony, but he talked to Roberto. He asked

89

Roberto what the songs were that they had sung. When Roberto named them, Grandpapa said, "Oh, yes. It goes like this," and he sang a line or two.

It was the same when Papa came in. Grandpapa talked to Papa. He talked to Papa about the things he knew that Papa liked to talk about.

"You are a charming guest," Mama told him. Grandpapa made her a little bow. "I pay my way with laughter, Doña," he spoke as if he were talking to a stranger, not to Mama. Mama spread her skirts out wide. She too made a little bow. "Thank you, Don Miguel Roberto. Thank you."

"Those two!" Papa said. Everyone laughed. Everyone felt gay and full of laughter. Tony forgot to be impatient. So the long day passed, with happiness asking the hours to dance with them.

Finally Grandpapa went home to sleep in his own bed and to waken in his own house. Tony went with him to dream away the night until another morning came.

With this new morning, Grandpapa's promise came true. "Well, Manuel Antonio," Grandpapa said smiling, "I have thought of something that you and I can make. Yes. I have thought of something just as I said I would."

Tony could not say a word. He just sat there with his eyes as round and as bright as two suns in the sky.

Grandpapa was very pleased with himself. He kept saying "Yes, sir, it takes me to think of things."

Grandpapa went to the door. He pointed to his ox-cart on the corredor. "See that ox-cart, Manuel Antonio?"

"Yes, Grandpapa."

"Close your eyes, young fellow. Can't you see it going down the road, proud in its lovely painted beauty, singing its harness song?

Can't you see it being pulled by two great oxen? Can't you, Manuel Antonio?"

"Yes, oh, yes!"

"Aha! Of course you can! Know what? Oxen and the cart they pull are a country man's riches. To young and old they mean one thing. They mean a proud possession."

Grandpapa looked at Tony. He seemed surprised that Tony did not know what the something-to-make was to be.

"Men have this great possession at least once in their lifetime. But children? Children never have it while they are children. We will fix that. We will give the children oxen and an ox-cart while they are young. It will be theirs to love, to care for, and to play with. We will make it small but perfect. We will make it out of wood."

"A toy, Grandpapa? A toy ox-cart and oxen for some little boy to play with? Oh, Grandpapa! Oh, Grandpapa!"

Tony began to dance around in great excitement. "Today, Grandpapa? Can we make it now?"

"Now. Today. Come, we will go for wood."

As they walked among the tall trees Grandpapa explained about the kinds of wood they needed. "In my young days my father was a great wheelmaker. He would not think of using any kind of wood except mahogany or that which we get from the guanacosta tree. But wheelmaking changes as the years change. Now people use the yellow alligator wood."

Grandpapa picked up a piece of wood that was lying on the ground. He ran his thumb along its side. He weighed it in his open hand. He smelled it. "So–oo," he said, thinking out loud. "This piece will do and this one here, I think."

They walked along, Grandpapa talking some more about ox-cart

making. "Yes, in my young days it was different. My father made the great cart wheels of one piece. Now they are made of sixteen pieces fitted together without a crack."

Grandpapa found another piece of wood. Soon he had what he thought would be enough, so they went back to his house. They carefully carried the wood they had found. It did not seem to be just wood now. It seemed to be two little oxen and a painted ox-cart.

Back at Grandpapa's house real work began. Grandpapa whittled and carved the wood. Tony helped in any way he could. He held the wood for his grandfather. He helped fit the pieces together. He cleaned the floor of all the long curls of shaving.

It took a long time to finish the something. Sometimes they put all the pieces away and rested or ate or slept or just sat still and thought of what was growing under Grandpapa's clever fingers.

"Let's keep it our surprise and not tell what we are doing until it is finished."

"Yes. That will be best, I think."

They had a hard time doing that because they had so many visitors. Mama and Papa came, and Roberto. All at different times, but for the same thing. They wanted to know what the something was.

Grandpapa and Tony teased them. Sometimes they would say, "No. No. It is nothing. We have nothing."

Sometimes they would say, "Yes, yes. It is something. We do have something."

All the time they would say, "Wait."

Finally it was finished. Two little oxen and a perfect little cart! Everything was right. Everything was perfect. "Now for the paint," Grandpapa said. "What are the colors we will need?"

"Black and white for the oxen. Like the ones you had before your last ox died."

"Yes, black and white for the oxen. What colors for the cart?"

"Well yours is—"

But Grandpapa said quickly. "This cart is your cart, so you must use your own design."

"Oh, Grandpapa! Do you mean it? I can make my own design? One that I can use on my own ox-cart when I am a man and have oxen and an ox-cart?"

"Yes, of course. Your own design."

"Will you help me make it?"

"I will show you how to use a ruler and a compass. I have here the ones that were my father's. I have used them and your Papa has used them. I will show you how to use them. The design must be your own. It must come from your head and your heart."

Then followed hours and hours and hours of drawing. Tony drew designs on every flat piece of wood he could find. At last he had what pleased him.

"It is not as good as your design, Grandpapa."

"It will be. Designs grow as their makers grow. They get better as the years go by."

After the designs were drawn on the four sides of the cart, the two wheels, the tiny ox yoke, the real problem came to worry them.

"Where will we get the paint?"

"Well, I myself have some black and a little red paint."

"My Papa has blue paint. He has blue paint in a can. I know he will let me have what I need."

"What other colors will you want?"

"Well, I will want yellow and white and green."

Just then there were noises outside the door. It sounded like many people coming. Grandpapa and Tony hurried to put the something away. Grandpapa went to the door. It had sounded like many people, and there were many people. There was Mama and Papa and Roberto, and who was that hiding behind the woodpile? Grandpapa and Tony went to look behind it.

It was—it could not be—but, yes, it was! It was Maria Rosita come home for a visit.

Such laughter! Such talk! Such happiness that followed. It was a long time before the family could settle down to quiet. Then Papa said, "We have come to see the something."

Grandpapa and Tony said, "Yes. It is not finished, but yes, we want you to see it."

Tony brought the little toy oxen and the little toy cart and put them on the table.

"Ay! Ay! Ay!" The family talked all at once. The family talked together. Their words ran around the room in little circles, bumping into one another as the circles of words grew larger.

Even Grandpapa could not stop them. He and Tony stood beside the oxen and listened to all the nice things the family were saying.

Finally it came time to talk about the paint.

"Yes, but of course," Papa said. "It would make me happy to give my blue paint.

"What other colors do you need?"

"Well, Papa will give me the blue and Grandpapa has black and a little red paint. I will need white and yellow and green."

"The Patron has much white paint. He has yellow too, I think. I will ask the Patron for white and yellow colors to give to you, Tony."

"Thank you, Roberto."

"And I will buy you paint brushes at San José."

"Thank you, Maria Rosita."

"Now I need green paint. Where can I get some green paint, Mama?"

Mama smiled at him. "I have no paint. No green or any other color." She was teasing. Tony knew it. He waited. Mama would help. She did. She said, "But I know how to get green paint for you, Manuel Antonio. I will show you how to mix blue and yellow together to make green."

"It does? You will? Thank you, Mama, thank you."

Mama wanted Grandpapa and Tony to come home with them, but they said, "No. We have too much work to do."

Grandpapa added, "We will paint the cart and the oxen quickly. Then we will bring them to show to you."

Tony said, "Even before it dries, we will bring it to you. We will carry it carefully."

The family said, "Yes. Yes. We will be waiting."

"Good-by then, until the oxen and the cart are painted."

"Good-by. Good-by."

11. A Day at the Market

THE oxen were painted. They were white with black patches. They had big black eyes that could almost see. They were matched except for a tiny black spot on one ox's side where Tony had dropped the paint brush. It had made an extra patch of black. Grandpapa said, "Let it stand as it is. Few things in this world are perfect."

The ox yoke was painted with a small design like the one on the ends of the cart. The cart had four designs. The two end ones were alike. The sides were alike. The wheels were beautiful. All the colors were on the wheels, blue and black and white, red and yellow and green. The green was just the right shade of green. Mama had mixed it, adding a bit of white and an even smaller bit of black to the blue and yellow paint.

"I'm going to mix all my colors next time," Tony said, "to see what colors I can get."

"You will see a color you won't want," Roberto told him.

Grandpapa and Tony had come to Mama's house now. The oxen and the ox-cart had the best place on the table. They were where Mama's vase of paper flowers had been. They were waiting for the paint to dry. It took a long time.

"It was almost dry before we left Grandpapa's house," Tony grumbled, sticking a little finger on the inside of the wheel. "Well, it's a little more than almost dry now."

"Tomorrow it will be very dry," Mama told him. "And tomorrow early, early, all of us will go to market with Manuel Antonio."

"Oh, thank you, Mama. Will you go too, Papa?"

"Of course I will go. Tomorrow will be an important day for this family. Tomorrow our good and brave Manuel Antonio takes his oxen to market."

"I must go back to Niña Lygia's tomorrow," said Maria Rosita, "but first there will be time to go with Tony to the market."

"I too am needed with you at market in the morning. I will take the milk on my way."

"Grandpapa, will you go?" But no, Grandpapa did not like to go to market. "I do not like to ride on the bus. If I had work that called me, it would be different. Then I would go."

Tony could not understand why anyone would not like to go to market. But then, Grandpapa was old. He had enjoyed many years of market days.

Grandpapa said he was going back to his house now. He said he liked his house. He liked to be there. "Come to tell me, Tony, what luck you had, and God be with you on your journey." Grandpapa went down the road and the family went back to their different work.

Papa was working in the cane field today. Roberto went up to the Patron's milking shed. Mama and Maria Rosita were busy getting all the things ready that they wanted to take to market in the morning. Mama sent Tony out to find eggs and flowers too. She told him, "I want two armfuls of those white flowers. They grow in the long grass beside the road."

"I can't find them. I don't know what they look like."

"You can find them by their heavy, sweet smell."

"I can't bring eggs and flowers at the same time."

"Bring them at different times. You have all the afternoon."

"Bring me orchids too," Maria Rosita called. "Bring me the little yellow ones. I want to sell them."

"Roberto will do that. He gathers purple orchids and puts them in little wire baskets."

"Mama, he just wants to stand there looking at his oxen." Maria Rosita sounded cross.

"I'm going, Mama." Tony spoke quickly before Mama could tell him to go. He took a long last look at the little ox-cart and the patient oxen standing on the table, waiting for their paint to dry.

He went outside into the wooded places to hunt for eggs and white flowers and orchids. After a while he began to enjoy his task. Doing things did help the long, long day to end.

And then it was morning. The family were ready for market. They were waiting at the road side for the bus to come.

"Today did come after all, Tony," Maria Rosita teased. She had so many flowers and so many orchids Papa kept saying, "I cannot find Maria Rosita. Where is she, Mama?"

"Today came all right, but it took yesterday a year to end, didn't it, Tony?" Roberto was teasing Maria Rosita now. He was helping Tony.

Tony looked at his big brother. "I never knew before how handsome you are, Roberto."

Just then the bus came and the family forgot their laughter in the noise and excitement of getting on the bus. At last they were crowded in. Papa and Roberto were carrying Maria Rosita's flowers. Mama and Rosita were crowded in the back seat with the hen and the beans and the eggs and the peas Mama was taking to market.

Tony sat in the aisle on a board placed between two seats. He

held his oxen and cart tightly in his arms. He had planned to sit
by the open bus window to watch the world go by. As it was, all
that he could see were pieces of people crowded closely around
him.

The bus lurched and swayed and bumped and rattled. "When
I'm an old man I won't go to market," Tony thought. He felt sleepy,
but he was afraid to sleep. His cart might fall. Tony looked down
at the floor of the bus. All that he could see were bare brown feet.
He stretched his eyes wide and clutched his cart tighter.

The bus stopped often, with more and more people crowding in
with ducks and chickens, flowers and baskets. Tony had a terrible
thought, "What if we are so packed in that we cannot move to get
out." He turned to find Mama or Papa or someone that he knew,

but all he could see were feet and arms and buckets and baskets.

Then the bus stopped and the people began getting out. Roberto picked him up and jumped him over the seat. Then he was outside. He was in San José! Mama and Papa, Roberto and Maria Rosita, were with him. The market was around the corner. Oh! How wonderful was everything! Tony put one hand in Roberto's strong one. With his other hand he held his ox-cart close to him so it would not get broken in the crowd.

Market at San José was many large buildings on both sides of the street. They were bigger than the sugar mill and the cane field. Inside they were cool and a little dark, and the narrow aisles between the booths were like animal trails among the trees at home.

At first the family looked at the people who were selling outside the market. Some had booths. There were flower booths and leather-goods booths and booths where bananas and mangoes, pineapples and other fruits, were sold. The country people sat near the edges of the sidewalks and spread what they had to sell around them. Mama saw some friends, so she sat with them, her hen and eggs and beans beside her. She began shelling the green peas she had brought from her garden. The rich ladies of the city liked to buy their green peas shelled.

Maria Rosita and Roberto went to the flower booths to sell their yellow and purple orchids and their white sweet-smelling flowers.

Papa and Tony stopped to look at saddles. They did not want to buy, they wanted to look. The saddles were leather with quilted seats and long leather skirts.

Maria Rosita and Roberto came. Mama was with them. "Now we are ready," Papa told Tony, "to go with you while you sell your oxen." Tony held his ox-cart closer to him. Now that the big moment had come he felt frightened.

The family went along the crowded sidewalks.

People were walking and pushing and crowding. The street was full of mule-carts and people and bicycles and here and there a truck or a bus or an automobile.

The family walked to the square, the little plaza. There the Christmas toy booths had been built. They looked into each one. They looked at the toys for sale and at the man who sold them. One booth had dolls and doll houses. One booth had wooden wagons and wooden trains. One booth had clowns on sticks and animals on little wheels.

And here was a booth with toy oxen and toy ox-carts. Tony looked at them. His lips pushed out, the way they did when he was thinking. The oxen were carved too thin. They were too long for oxen. The wood used was not right. It was balsa wood. Who ever heard of an ox-cart made of balsa wood! No! Tony turned away. Not that booth! Never in the world would he let his beautiful oxen stand for sale with oxen of poor quality. Never!

The family walked along. They saw a booth where footballs and rubber balls were sold. Tony stood a long time looking at the footballs. He would like to have one. He sighed. Someday, perhaps, he could. Not now. He turned away. The family followed.

Roberto pointed. "Here is another toy ox booth."

Tony looked. The oxen and carts were better here. Not so good as his, perhaps, but better than at the other booth. Yes, this might be the place. Tony planned to say, "Good morning, Señor. You are buying oxen and carts, perhaps? Perhaps you will buy mine? It is beautifully carved. Notice the wood, yellow alligator it is. The design, Señor, the design is my design, and the paint, all the colors are there. Even the green, Señor, that my Mama made from blue and yellow with a bit of white and a smaller bit of black."

Yes. Tony knew what he would say. He had thought it out word by word for many days. He knew just what he would say. He had not forgotten. He was ready.

Tony held the ox-cart out. He raised his eyes to look at the man who stood there. "No," Tony decided and turned away. His ox-cart was not for sale at this place.

"Why?" Mama's voice was soft and kind. "Why? Can you tell us."

"That man," Tony began. "That man, his face—it was not kind."

"Let's eat," Roberto said. "Let's go to the resting place where the country people are. Let's eat."

The family walked along. They understood. Tony loved them very much.

They turned into a quiet street that led to the resting place where the oxen were kept to rest before they went back home again at evening time.

Two ladies were walking toward them. Anyone could tell they were not Costa Rican ladies. They were not so beautiful, for one thing. They wore flat-heeled shoes, not high-heeled pointed slippers like the rich ladies of Costa Rica. They wore hats. Tony almost laughed. He would have if he had not been so polite. The ladies stopped. One of them had blue eyes. She pointed to Tony's cart. She spoke to him in Spanish. Her Spanish sounded funny. "She is North American," Maria Rosita whispered.

The North American lady said in Spanish, "Your cart is beautiful. I would like to buy it if it is for sale."

Tony nodded his head. All his carefully learned speech was forgotten.

"I would like to buy it." The lady's voice was kind. It made her poor Spanish seem not so funny. "What do you want me to pay you for it?"

Tony could not say a word. He wanted very much to speak, but no words came.

Then Papa helped him. "It is Tony's to sell, of course. But I think he would like to say that whatever you would like to pay will be right."

Tony nodded his head. Yes, that was what he would have liked to say. The lady spoke in English to her friend. "A colon, a piece of Costa Rican money or a Costa Rican dollar, is worth eighteen

cents. Three times eighteen is fifty-four cents. Would that be enough?"

"Better make it six colones," her friend told her, also in English. "A dollar is fair, I think."

The blue-eyed North American handed Tony six colones. Mama and Papa, Maria Rosita and Roberto, crowded around. Six colones! Too much! But then, if that was what they wanted to pay! Papa lifted his shoulders high and Mama lifted her hands. Maria Rosita and Roberto said, "Yes, yes. Thank you. Thank you."

Tony stood with the money in his hand. At first he could think of nothing except that his oxen were his no more. They did not belong to him now. They belonged to a strange lady with beautiful blue eyes.

The ladies said good-by. They went down the street taking with them the painted oxen and the ox-cart.

The family were looking at Tony's money. "Six colones! Six colones! Think of it!"

A wave of joy washed Tony's grief away. He looked at the money in his hand. "Money!"

His dream had come true. Now he could buy what he had dreamed of buying.

With a sob he threw himself into Mama's arms.

12. Money Can Be Magic

THE family had eaten the "roosters" that Mama had brought for them. They had met some friends at the courtyard where the oxen were resting and had sat in the shade near by, and visited. To others they had said *adios* as they passed by, in the friendly Costa Rican way.

Now they were back in the market streets again. It was as busy and as crowded as it had been earlier in the day. This surprised Tony. He had thought that, because his family had gone away to do other things, to eat their lunch, to rest a bit, to talk with friends, everyone else would have gone away. It disappointed him to know that buying and selling kept on. If he was there, it added one small boy to the crowded street. If he was not there, market kept on, just the same as it was every day.

Maria Rosita stopped to look at pretty combs for her hair. There were all kinds, red ones with white beads, blue ones with pink beads. Mama liked them too, not for herself, but for Rosita.

Rosita said, "Someday when I have made more money working at Niña Lygia's house, I will buy some combs. The girls here wear them."

Rosita looked at her pretty shoes. She was wearing them, now that she was back in San José. She said to Mama, "Papa was good to me to buy these slippers that day when he had money." Maria Rosita looked hopefully at Tony.

Tony did not see her. He was looking into little mirrors that were for sale, next to the pretty combs. He heard, perhaps, but he did not understand. He was making faces in the mirrors.

Mama also looked at Tony. She shrugged her shoulders. "Our Tony is very like his Papa," she told her pretty daughter. "He has doors in his ears and eyes."

"And keys to his pocket," Maria Rosita said laughingly.

The family stopped at another booth. This place had nothing but straw hats for sale. Roberto tried on a very gay one. It had red and black and blue straw woven into a design. "A fine hat, that one," the hat man said to Roberto. "It comes from Ecuador."

"From Ecuador! Think of that! To wear a hat from Ecuador." Roberto waited. "Well," he said, taking the hat off and giving it back to the man, "who would wear a hat from Ecuador!"

The family walked on. Papa saw some saddlebags. "Good work in these," he told Roberto. "Someday I want you to have good saddlebags to put behind your saddle when you ride for the Patron."

Papa said to the man, "What is the too high price you ask for these?"

"Five colones, and cheap for that money."

"So–oo?" Papa sounded just like Grandpapa.

Mama and Rosita were fingering a lace mantilla. "You need this for church on Sunday, Maria Rosita."

"Yes, Mama, I do."

"Well someday—"

"Yes, Mama, someday."

They had come to the football booth again. Tony was looking at one of the beautiful balls. He just looked at it. He knew how it would feel in his hands. He did not need to touch it. He knew how

it would fly over the grassy football field. He had always wanted
a football. Now it was here. He could have it. He could say, "Ah,
Señor, the football there. I would have it, please. The money?
Certainly. Here is the money, Señor." He would take the football.
He would carry it home on the bus. Tomorrow when the boys came
by to play he would show it to them.

Tony turned away. He put his hand in his Papa's strong one.

"It is difficult to keep money when you have it, isn't it, Papa?"
he asked.

Papa held his hand tightly. He nodded. "It is as hard to keep it
as it is to get it." Papa snapped his fingers, "Money! It can do
strange things," he said.

Maria Rosita had stopped at a candy cart. Here on trays were
all kinds of little candies. Some were red roses on a thumb-sized
green leaf. Some were apples. One tray had little birds, blue birds
and red birds. Maria Rosita looked at them a long time. Finally
she chose five, all different kinds, all different colors. She untied
the corner of her handkerchief and gave the candy man five small
pieces of copper money. She passed the candy around to her family. "I am treating you to candy," she said.

The candy was beautiful. Tony did not want to eat his, it was
so pretty. Finally, he put it in his mouth, but not to bite it. Just to
let it stay there on his tongue, getting smaller and smaller, but
staying beautiful until the last minute when it melted away.

"Now it is my turn," Roberto told them. He held his hand up
like a grand señor to tell the ice-cream vendor to bring his cart.
Roberto talked to the vendor a long time. He asked him many
questions. Was the ice cream cold and not soft? Was it made of
good milk? What flavors did he have for sale? How large were the
ice-cream cones? How much?

Roberto chose the flavors, one cone of red ice cream, one cone of yellow, one of orange, one of white, and the last one chocolate. He counted the money he took from his pocket. He counted it carefully. He put one money piece away and gave the rest to the ice-cream vendor.

Roberto held the ice-cream cones. They looked like flowers in his hands. He gave his family their choice. Then Roberto took the last one. It was white.

Roberto told Tony, "Do not bite into it. It is too cold that way."

"Besides," Maria Rosita added, "to bite it makes it go too quickly."

The family ate the ice cream as they walked along looking at everything.

Mama bought a lamp chimney and a bottle of kerosene.

Papa bought a présent for Mama, a blue glass vase. It was lovely. Everyone handled it and looked at it. Tony looked through it at the sun. It made the sun a dark blue color.

Mama said, "Thank you, Papa. You are a good man." Mama touched the blue vase gently. You could see that she liked it very much. "I will give my other one to Grandpapa. He can put it on his table."

"And I will make him crepe-paper flowers to put in it. I will bring them with me when I come home again."

Papa said, "You are a good girl, Maria Rosita."

Papa and Mama talked together. They counted Mama's money. Papa said, "Yes, there is enough. We will have some soda pop. Mama and I will buy it."

Roberto laughed. "Everybody is feeling rich today."

Papa came back with red pop in blue-green bottles. The family sat down on the edge of the sidewalk with the other sitting people. They sat there to rest, to drink the pop, and to watch the people go by.

The market was as crowded as ever. Rich ladies walked by, choosing the vegetables they wanted to buy. Their little maids walked with them. They put the vegetables in baskets and gave them to the little errand boys to carry.

Tony did not drink all of his pop.

"Don't you like it?" Papa asked him.

"I am saving it to take home to Grandpapa."

"Ay! Ay! That is good. We will help fill the bottle again."

Everyone put some pop into Tony's bottle until it was full again. Roberto put the stopper on. It looked new. Grandpapa would be pleased.

A red mule-cart filled high with pineapples stopped near where the family were sitting. The mule was not well trained. It would not stand still while its owner unloaded the cart. The man was cross. He shouted at his mule.

Tony went to help him. "Señor, I will hold this mule for you," he said politely.

"Good," the man said. "This mule comes from Nicaragua. I have bought him but yesterday. He is not trained."

"He is a beautiful mule." Tony looked at the mule's short-cut mane. It was yellow-gray and black in checks. It was different from any mule that Tony had ever seen.

"Thank you for helping me," the man said when he had unloaded all of his pineapples. "Here is one for you."

"Thank you, Señor. Thank you very much."

Tony went back to the sidewalk where his family was waiting for him. "My treat to you," he told them grandly. Papa cut the pineapple with his machete. Then he sliced it in thick juicy slices. It tasted good.

Maria Rosita finally said, "Well, it is time I went to Niña Lygia's house."

"What are you buying with your money, Tony?" Mama looked at her little boy. All the family looked at him. Tony held his money tighter. It had not been out of his hand. Even when he held the mule for the señor, he also had held his money.

"Is it still a secret?" Papa asked him.

"It is something for Grandpapa."

"Can't you buy it at the market? We can help you."

Tony shook his head. "It is something for Grandpapa," was all he said.

Maria Rosita stood up. "I must go. Niña Lygia will not like it if I do not come now. It is late."

All the family stood up. "We will walk with you to Niña Lygia's house," they told her.

They went to Niña Lygia's house. They went in. Tony had not known that houses could be so beautiful. He held his money tighter. Somehow he felt less frightened at so much beauty, now that he too was a man with money in his possession.

Niña Lygia was as gracious as she was lovely. She welcomed Maria Rosita back again. She did not scold her because the hour was late. She told Rosita to take her family to the kitchen, to give them coffee and sweet rolls and oatmeal milk sweetened with brown sugar. Niña Lygia herself came into the kitchen. She talked with Mama and with Papa. She smiled at Roberto and Tony.

After a time Mama said that they must go. They thanked Niña Lygia. They said good-by to Rosita. They went to find the bus to take them home.

The bus was waiting. It was almost empty. They got good seats. Even Tony got a seat next to the window.

"When does this bus leave?" Papa asked the man who drove the bus. Papa knew, but he asked just the same. The man shrugged his shoulders. "When the people come to fill it up," he said. "Who knows? Maybe an hour. Maybe now. When it is filled, we go."

Papa was pleased. The man had said what he thought he would.

The few people in the bus sat quietly. They were tired. They were ready to go home.

"You can see everything from the window, Tony," Papa said.

"You can sleep as we ride along," Mama said.

Tony did not answer. He was thinking. He was filled with quiet happiness. He had the money. He had not lost it. He had not spent it. He had it with him. As soon as he got home he could tell the secret to Grandpapa.

Oh, happy day! Oh, happy day that made a dream come true!

The bus was filling quickly now. The people were coming faster. At last the bus was full. The people were crowded together. They were sitting on little boards between the seats in the aisle. They were standing in front.

The bus started. It roared through the streets. It passed the marketplace. It passed the glass factory where Mama's blue vase had been made. It went along the road into the country, farther and farther into the country. Now the trees were growing by the road.

Tony sat quietly, looking out the window, holding the money tightly in his hand and thinking about his secret.

At last the bus came to their stop. They got off. They were at home. Tony ran down the little narrow road to Grandpapa's house.

The old man was sitting at his supper table. He was eating rice and beans and drinking coffee. When Tony came into the room, he pushed his plate and cup away. He looked at Tony.

Tony's cheeks were red, red with excitement. His eyes were shining brighter than lamplight. He was out of breath. He was talking quickly, as fast as his Mama did when she was very pleased.

"Grandpapa! Grandpapa! A lady bought it. A lady bought the cart and oxen. She gave me money. I have it. I did not spend it. I did not buy a football."

Grandpapa made Tony sit down. He listened while Tony told all that had happened—everything. He did not forget a thing. He gave his Grandpapa the soda pop that he had brought for him. At last he had finished. He had told all that had happened. He had told almost all. Now there was one thing left.

"This is the money. This is for you, my precious Grandpapa." Tony's voice was low now. He was almost whispering. He could

hear his own heart beating. It was singing. It was singing louder than he could make his words come out.

"This money—it is for you to buy two great white oxen. Two great white oxen, Grandpapa, to pull your cart again to the sugar-cane field."

"Tony," Grandpapa said. "Tony, Tony! You did this for me?"

Grandpapa looked at the money. How could he tell Tony that six colones could not buy oxen. It was not enough, not enough by a hundred times. How could he tell him? Tony knew money only as money. There had never been enough in his small world to know that a little money buys little things and that it takes big money to buy bigger things.

Tony was talking. "Tomorrow, Grandpapa, you can go tomorrow to buy your two white oxen."

"Tony, Tony! Money is not just money, my little boy. It first must be how big, how many, and then, how much. Six colones is not enough to buy two white oxen."

"Not enough, Grandpapa? Not enough? Not big enough?"

Grandpapa shook his head. He could not speak. He was crying.

"Can't money do everything, Grandpapa? Isn't money magic like Roberto is always saying? Isn't money magic, Grandpapa?"

Again Grandpapa shook his head. His old voice sounded broken, like Mama's blue glass vase would sound if one dropped it on a stone.

"Money is not magic," Grandpapa began and then something seemed to happen to him. He seemed taller. He seemed younger. His voice was strong, not broken now. It was almost like a song.

"Tony—" Even the creeping shadows in the room stood still, listening. "Tony, money can be magic. It is what it makes you do. Yes. Yes. Yes. Money can be magic. Good magic. See what it has done to me? You saw me old, but now I am not old. I am young. My thinking and my heart is young again. I will not sit here weeping because I can no longer lead the others in the cane field. No. I will work again. You and I will be partners in a business. We will make toy oxen and toy ox-carts. We will sell them at the market. We will save the money."

Grandpapa took the six colones. He found a can to put them in. "When this can is full, my Tony, you and I will buy our oxen, our two great white oxen."

"Our oxen, Grandpapa?"

"Our oxen, Tony. Soon too, I know it. My heart tells me it will be soon. Every Saturday we will go to market with our toy oxen to sell. Yes, Tony. Maybe we will have two, three, four to sell. Who knows how many? Who knows how much money they will bring?"

"Oh, Grandpapa, money is magic!"

"Money can be magic."

A knock came at the door. It was Papa with his lantern.

"Tomorrow," Grandpapa told him, "tomorrow we will tell you about our business, but tonight—" Grandpapa's voice softened— "tonight a tired boy must sleep."

Tony's eyes asked, "Tomorrow?"

Grandpapa's eyes promised, "Tomorrow."

Papa said, "Come. I have brought my lantern to guide you safely home."

Grandpapa stood at his door and watched Papa and Tony go down the narrow ribbon of road to Tony's house.